RAZORBILL

No Such Thing as

Forever

Real love.

Real life.

The real thing . . .

www.girlheartboy.com

Coming soon

GIRL HEART BOY:
GIRLS' NIGHT IN

GIRL HEART BOY:
FORGET ME NOT
exclusive ebook short stories

and

GIRL HEART BOY:
RUMOUR HAS IT
in paperback and ebook

No Such Thing as
Forever

ALI CRONIN

razor
bill

PENGUIN

RAZORBILL

Published by the Penguin Group
Penguin Books Ltd, 80 Strand, London WC2R ORL, England
Penguin Group (USA) Inc., 375 Hudson Street, New York, New York 10014, USA
Penguin Group (Canada), 90 Eglinton Avenue East, Suite 700, Toronto, Ontario, Canada M4P 2Y3
(a division of Pearson Penguin Canada Inc.)
Penguin Ireland, 25 St Stephen's Green, Dublin 2, Ireland (a division of Penguin Books Ltd)
Penguin Group (Australia), 250 Camberwell Road, Camberwell, Victoria 3124, Australia
(a division of Pearson Australia Group Pty Ltd)
Penguin Books India Pvt Ltd, 11 Community Centre, Panchsheel Park, New Delhi – 110 017, India
Penguin Group (NZ), 67 Apollo Drive, Rosedale, Auckland 0632, New Zealand
(a division of Pearson New Zealand Ltd)
Penguin Books (South Africa) (Pty) Ltd, Block D, Rosebank Office Park, 181 Jan Smuts Avenue,
Parktown North, Gauteng 2193, South Africa

Penguin Books Ltd, Registered Offices: 80 Strand, London WC2R ORL, England

penguin.com

First published in Razorbill, an imprint of Penguin Books Ltd, 2012
001 – 10 9 8 7 6 5 4 3 2 1

Copyright © Penguin Books Ltd, 2012
All rights reserved

The moral right of the author has been asserted

Set in 13/15.25 pt Garamond MT Std
Typeset by Palimpsest Book Production Limited, Falkirk, Stirlingshire
Printed in Great Britain by Clays Ltd, St Ives plc

British Library Cataloguing in Publication Data
A CIP catalogue record for this book is available from the British Library

ISBN: 978–0–141–34425–6

www.greenpenguin.co.uk

Penguin Books is committed to a sustainable
future for our business, our readers and our planet.
This book is made from Forest Stewardship
Council™ certified paper.

MIX
Paper from
responsible sources
FSC™ C018179
www.fsc.org

ALWAYS LEARNING   PEARSON

For my family

1

Ashley stretched like a cat and yawned so wide I could see the flappy bit at the back of her throat.

'Yeah, no, I dunno,' she said, post-yawn. 'Maybe four? No wait . . .' She looked at the common-room ceiling, as if the mounds of gobbed paper stuck there would provide some insight into her holiday sex stats. 'Yeah. Four.' She scratched at her eyebrow ring. Lovely Ashley and her insatiable need to be edgy.

I wriggled on my chair. Partly because although it was September it was bloody boiling, and scratchy common-room chairs + sweaty thighs = not comfy. But also because I had a secret. Well, it wasn't a secret, but at the same time I didn't want just to shout it out. A girl has standards.

Donna gave Ashley a little round of applause. 'Nice work, lady. So, to recap. Zero for me . . .' She raised the back of her hand to her forehead in mock regret. 'Obviously just the one for Ms Monogamy over here.'

Cass smiled almost guiltily and hugged her knees. Bless her, after nearly four years with Adam she knows the score. Let's just say he's not exactly Mr Monogamy.

'Which just leaves our feminist friend, Sarah.' Donna plonked herself on my knee and hooked her arm round my neck.

'Any news, hmm?' she asked, pressing her cheek against mine and fluttering her eyelashes. She wears so much mascara I could feel a draught. I pushed her off. She was pretty heavy.

'That would be telling,' I said demurely, but I couldn't help grinning. Honestly, I'm such a tit.

Donna spun round from her position at my feet and looked up at me, her dark eyes enormous. 'Oh my God, you totally did it!'

I actually giggled. I know: tragic.

Ash and Cass both leant forward in their chairs like I was about to impart the news of the century, and I found myself with three pairs of eyes boring into me and three pairs of eyebrows reaching for the skies.

'What?'

Ash growled and chucked her apple core at me. 'Just tell us!'

'Well, his name's Joe . . .' I started, but was drowned out by my friends' shrieks. There was a split second when the room went silent and everyone turned to look at us, but it was over as soon as it had begun. It was the first day of term: it was not the first gossip-related shrieking incident.

'I KNEW there was something going on,' crowed Cass gleefully. 'You've been bouncing around like Tigger ever since we got here.'

Donna punched me affectionately on the arm. 'Who'd have thought, our own little man-hater's all growed up.'

'Ow! Piss off,' I said amiably, rubbing my arm. 'Anyway, I don't hate men.'

'So what happened?' asked Cass, rubbing her hands together at the thought of the juicy goss I was about to serve up.

So I told them.

It started with a Disney Princess football.

We were in Spain on holiday, me, my mum and dad and my little brother, Daniel. He's twelve and on the cusp of being a total dickhead, so I was keen to stay out of his way. In fact, my plan was to sunbathe, read, swim, eat and maybe do a bit of sightseeing and shopping. That's it. I mean, I liked my parents. I generally enjoyed being with them. But what they wanted from a holiday and what I wanted from a holiday was about as far apart as, let's say for argument's sake, getting up early to visit ancient ruins, and sleeping till noon to muster the energy for a busy afternoon's lazing. In short, I wasn't overly enthusiastic.

The first three days we all mooched about on the beach, my parents making a show of taking my needs into consideration, but then the call of scenery became too much and they took Dan (sucker!) in the hire car up some mountains to take photos of The View, while I took myself, my iPod and my book down to the beach for some serious doing-nothing.

I laid out my towel, rubbed Factor 30 into my exposed bits and settled down to some boy-meets-girl with an Ellie Goulding soundtrack. It was lovely to be basking in the sun, all on my own. I thought about the crisps and chocolate chilling in the cool bag beside me. Mum and Dad were of the opinion that eating anything between meals was some kind of character flaw. Like it was noble to be weak with hunger by teatime. But they weren't here to disapprove. I wriggled with contentment. And then a football shot out of nowhere and bounced off my sunglasses, popping out both lenses.

'OW! What the . . . ?' I howled, grabbing my poor broken shades. They were only Primark, but that wasn't the point. I looked up to see someone looming over me. The sun was in my eyes, but I could see that it was a boy, about my age, and that he didn't look particularly sorry.

'What the hell are you doing? That bloody hurt!' I had turned a fetching shade of beetroot, partly from the shock and the pain, but mainly cos I don't do confrontation. Irritable tutting is about as far as I go, but I was so angry it had just come out.

'I'm really sorry, mate,' he said, laughing. 'It was an accident. Ben's a donkey in midfield.' He pointed back at three guys, all pointing and laughing at me. Brilliant.

'Yeah, well, you could have blinded me,' I grumped.

'No offence, but I don't think so,' said the boy, still smirking. What was he so chirpy about? 'It's just plastic. Look.'

He held out the ball to me. It had Disney Princesses on it. And, while I didn't fall for him there and then, it was definitely the beginning.

Well, obviously I couldn't help smiling. 'Nice ball,' I said. Then blushed again, as I fought the urge to glance at his pant region.

He kneed the ball into the air and did a couple of keepy-uppies. 'Thanks. I found it.'

'Cool. Lucky you,' I said wittily.

He put his head on one side as if to say, 'Huh. Strange girl,' but then, despite my lack of conversational skills, flopped down on the sand beside me.

'I'm Joe,' he said.

'Hi, Joe.' He stared at me for a moment. I gawped

back at him. Oh shit. Right. Social niceties. 'Sarah,' I said hurriedly.

'Well, nice to meet you, Sarah,' he said, smiling again. He had ridiculously perfect teeth, which explained all the grinning. Show-off. He looked down to brush a fly off his foot and I took the chance to give him the once-over. Short light-brown hair that had gone all surfer stiff with sea spray, dark-brown eyes, slim but not skinny, and wearing nothing but loose swim shorts. There was no denying it: he was hot.

'So, you here on your own?' he asked, tossing the ball from hand to hand.

I shook my head. 'With my parents,' and then added quickly, 'but I pretty much do my own thing. How about you?'

'I'm with them,' said Joe, nodding back at his friends, who were now engrossed in pushing each other over in the sand. 'Mates from uni.'

We watched one of them clutch his chest and die in dramatic slow-motion under a volley of imaginary machine-gun fire from another, and I raised an eyebrow.

'Oh yeah, studying what?' I said. 'Arsing Around 101?' (Get me, making conversation! As long as his friends stayed over there, I'd be OK. I could handle a new person, but new people, plural? It was like my

6

worst nightmare. I didn't know what to do, what to say – even how to stand. Should I put my hands behind my back? Should I fold them? What expression should I have on my face? See? Nightmare. So instead I'd just clam up. It's probably where the man-hater rep came from. People mistook my social crapness for aloofness.)

Anyway, glory be, cos Joe laughed! 'Yeah, with Advanced Dick Studies,' he said. And then it was his turn to blush, or was it my imagination? 'I mean, not literally, y'know . . . studying dicks.'

I laughed then. 'It's OK. I knew what you meant.'

'Cool.' He met my eyes for a moment and smiled that smile again.

Despite myself, I felt a flutter of excitement. Here I was – me, the virgin queen! – sitting on a Spanish beach chatting with a boy who was both gorgeous and funny, and who had just looked deep into my eyes. The girls would never believe this. Hell, *I* could hardly believe it. I hated being a virgin among, well, a whole heap of non-virgins. Hated it. But at the same time I'd pretty much resigned myself to staying that way forever. The thought of a boy fancying me enough to want to do *It* with me was just . . . weird.

It's not as if I had self-esteem issues. I didn't spend hours in front of the mirror hating my body; I didn't wear much make-up; and I had ambition. I wanted to be a writer when I was older and had every intention of making it. Like, give me half an hour to stare into space and imagine my future self doing a book-signing in Waterstones and I was there. But myself in a sex-based scenario? Way less believable. Go figure.

'. . . anyway, join us if you fancy it.' Joe looked at me expectantly. Shit, I'd been so busy analysing our conversation I'd forgotten to actually engage with it (story of my life).

'Sorry, say that again?'

He gave me the *strange-girl alert* look again and said, 'We're having a barbecue on the beach tonight. Wondered if you wanted to come?'

'Oh yeah. Cool. Definitely.' Mercifully I stopped just short of adding, 'I'll ask my mum.'

Joe jumped to his feet and brushed the sand off his bum. 'OK, great. See you here, nine-ish.'

And with that he grabbed his princess ball and ran off to continue kicking Cinderella repeatedly in the face.

Over lunch that afternoon I brought up my plans for the evening.

'So, I was thinking of going out tonight,' I said, casually spooning potatoes on to my plate.

I felt my parents' eyes on me. 'Oh yes, who with?' asked Dad, cutting to the chase, as is his way.

'Just some people I met on the beach.'

'People . . . or *boys*?' Dad widened his eyes and waggled his fingers.

'*Boys* . . .' I hammed it up, mirroring him. 'But don't worry, they're my age.'

Dad squirted sauce on to his steak. 'Oh right, I'm not worried at all then.' He and Mum smirked at each other. I hated it when they did that *Ooh, look at our teenager playing at grown-ups* stuff.

I rolled my eyes. 'Well, we were planning on having a massive orgy, but if it'll make you feel better we'll just go to the beach for a barbecue.'

'What's an orgy?' piped up Dan.

'That's fine,' said Mum, ignoring him. 'Just don't be back too late. And don't get drunk.' She and Dad exchanged smiles again. Oh, how amusing to have a teenage daughter who caused you no trouble. *Just watch it*, I thought. *All that could change.*

That evening I stumbled down the path to the beach with butterflies in my stomach and fake tan on my legs. I'd spent a stupid amount of time choosing what to wear, from the ridiculously underdressed (swimming costume and sarong) to the plain ridiculous (heels). I finally settled on an H&M sundress with flip-flops and my mum's pashmina for warmth. Not exactly cutting edge, but then I'm no fashionista.

When I got to the beach the light was just beginning to fade, and I stopped for a moment to watch this strange boy who, even stranger, had apparently taken an interest in me. He was sitting on the sand, light from the setting sun giving him a kind of bronze glow. He was looking out to sea and occasionally swigging from a bottle of beer. His mates were messing about in the water, their shouts and laughter ebbing and flowing like the sea. But Joe was content to sit and just . . . be.

And ping! I fell for him. In the time it takes for a signal to move from eye to brain, I had transformed from a woefully inexperienced seventeen-year-old with stupidly high standards to one who had just been waiting for the right person. I almost laughed. I took a deep breath and set off down the beach, my flip-flops sliding around in the sand so my sophisticated sashay turned into an attractive drunken lurch.

'Sarah, hey!' said Joe, jumping up and kissing my cheek. He was a bit stubbly, and he smelled lovely. Sort of fresh and cucumber-y.

'Sit down. Drink?' he said, offering me a beer, which I hate but I took one anyway. I looked around for the barbecue.

'Turns out they enforce the "No Barbecues" thing,' said Joe, reading my mind. 'We got ours confiscated.'

He jutted out his lip petulantly like a little kid, and I'm sorry, but it was cute.

'How come you're not with your friends?' I asked, taking a sip of beer and wincing. Joe looked at me.

'You don't like it, do you?' he said, smiling.

'Not really,' I admitted.

'Here, I'll have it.' His hand brushed mine as he took the bottle. 'There's a couple of Cokes in there, I think.' He nodded at a supermarket carrier bag.

'Thanks,' I said, taking one and clinking his bottle with it. 'Cheers.'

'Cheers to you too, Sarah Doesn't-like-beer.'

'So, how come you're not swimming?' I asked again.

Joe looked down at the sand and smiled, then lifted his eyes to mine. 'Because I have good friends,' he said cryptically.

'Oh. Right. Cool,' I said, not wanting to presume. Although I totally was presuming. Had they really left him so we could be alone?

Joe didn't move his eyes away from mine, and I could feel my face getting hot. 'You're quite beautiful, aren't you?' he said simply. I presumed it was a rhetorical question. What was I supposed to say? '*Well, as you can clearly see, I'm not actually beautiful. In the right light I am quite pretty, though*'? I kept quiet, and smiled goofily. Turns out even if you know a compliment isn't true, hearing it can make your heart sing. I took a mouthful of Coke for something to do besides grin inanely.

With his eyes on my lips, Joe moved his face towards mine. I'd like to say that our lips met in a passionate kiss while the waves crashed symbolically in front of us. But actually I choked on my drink.

'Oh God,' I said when I'd finally finished spluttering. 'That was not supposed to happen.' I dared to look at Joe, but, instead of regarding me with the disgust I deserved, his eyes were twinkling with what seemed suspiciously like affection. He put his hand gently behind my head.

'Come here, you,' he said, and pulled me towards him.

Cue kiss.

2

And cue further screaming from the girls back in the common room.

'Oh my God, what was it like?' asked Cass, her eyes shining as she clasped her hands in rapture.

'Never mind that,' said Donna. 'When's the sex part?'

'It was lovely,' I said, smiling as I remembered the way Joe stroked my face and ran his other hand up through my hair at the nape of my neck. Lovely didn't cover it. It was bliss – pure and simple – and it made me feel gorgeous and sexy and special.

'Aw, look at her,' crooned Ashley, reaching out to tuck a loose strand of hair behind my ear. 'She's in lurve.'

'Shuddup, Ash,' I said, trying to ignore the heart-based fluttering that happened whenever I thought about Joe.

'Anyway,' said Donna, making winding-up movements with her hands. 'The sex . . . ?'

'All in good time, young Donna,' I said primly. 'A lady waits, you know.'

Ashley snorted. 'Sod that. A lady gets it when she wants it.' Me and Cass looked at each other and rolled our eyes. This was a favourite theme of Ashley's.

'Mark of a true feminist,' she said, picking at a hangnail on her big toe.

'Yeah, all right, keep your Birkenstocks on,' said Cass, ignoring the one-finger salute she got in return. 'Go on, hon.'

But the beeps for next period put paid to any more revelations. With a promise to meet back in the common room at lunch, we went our separate ways. Me to English, Cass to politics, Donna to theatre studies and Ash to media studies. Not that we knew each other's timetables or anything.

Actually we knew everything about each other, more or less, and had done since the first week of Year Seven. You know how when you start a new school you hook up with people pretty quickly but only find your real friends over time? That didn't happen with us. We found each other straight away, as if it was meant to be.

We were put on the same table in science on our second day at school. Cass and Donna had been at the same primary school, although they'd never really spoken, but otherwise we didn't know each other at all. My best friend from primary school,

Megan Roberts, had emigrated to Australia in the summer holidays, and I was properly grieving. I felt like half of me was missing and I didn't really care who I sat next to. Anyway, we didn't get a choice cos our teacher, Mr Evershot, placed us.

It was my policy to instantly hate any teacher who didn't let us choose our own seats or partners in group work, but you couldn't hate Mr Evershot because he was tiny like a gnome and nice without being try-hard. He had a *really* strong northern accent. He was from Wakefield in Yorkshire. I know this because we saw it written on the board when we got into class that first day. 'Mr Evershot. From Wakefield in Yorkshire.' Some boy had shouted out, 'Is that why you talk funny, sir?' and Mr Evershot had just looked him in the eye and said, 'Yep.' That shut him up.

Anyway. There we were: Donna and Cass all uncomfortable because even though they'd gone to the same school they'd hardly spoken and definitely never sat next to each other; Ashley chewing the skin off the side of her nails and scowling because her mum had just finished with a boyfriend who Ash had really liked; and me feeling miserable and awkward. On paper, not exactly a match made in heaven.

But then Mr Evershot made us break off into groups to discuss what the most dangerous room in the house was (Year Seven science for you), so we were forced to talk to each other.

'Well, obviously it's the kitchen,' said Ashley, who I was instantly terrified of because she was chewing gum in class and sounded bored (it didn't take much to freak me out back then).

'So let's say living room,' said Donna. 'To be original.'

Ash must have approved of that, although I don't remember what she said, but Cass piped up with: 'I don't think we get extra points for being different. It's more a right/wrong scenario.' I still remember the way her voice sounded: sort of sweet and gentle, like she was genuinely trying to help. I was eaten up with admiration that she'd (a) stood up to Donna, who had a rougher accent than mine and was therefore – yes – scary and (b) used the word 'scenario'.

So we were at least talking, though nobody could accuse us of instantly clicking. But then the Defining Moment of our friendship: Mr Evershot stumbled as he walked past our desk and whispered, 'Fook,' under his breath.

And the four of us cracked up. A teacher saying a rude word was funny enough, but a teacher saying a rude word in an accent? We were crying with laughter. Honking and wheezing like a bunch of asthmatic geese. After a minute we'd calm down, but then one of us would catch another's eye and it'd start all over again.

'Something funny, girls?' Mr Evershot had asked wryly, but he didn't tell us off, adding instead: 'Glad to see you're getting on, but make sure you come up with the goods.' He pointed at the piece of paper in front of us and we eyed each other and giggled, but got back to listing dangerous household appliances.

And you can't really not be friends after that. Soon we started going to lunch after the lesson, and it went from there. We were only eleven years old then. Just kids. Most of us hadn't even started our periods.

And now here we were, still best friends and about to go into the big wide world together.

But first I had to go to English, Cass to politics, Donna to theatre studies and Ash to media studies . . .

3

'So. Appearance and reality in *Jane Eyre* . . . Thank you, Mr Jones.'

Mr Roberts handed my friend Rich a bunch of papers to hand out. I loved *Jane Eyre*, but Mr Roberts had the uncanny knack of turning any book into the most brain-bangingly dull story ever written. He also insisted on being called Mr Roberts, in return for which he called us all Mr or Miss Whatever. He thought he was single-handedly maintaining traditional values while treating us with the kind of respect that we, as upper-school students, deserved. We thought he was a dick.

Anyway, I'd read *Jane Eyre*, like, five times so I happily zoned out. I didn't quite gaze out of the window with a secret smile playing about my lips while absently doodling love hearts with Joe's initials in them, but it was close.

I so didn't want to be the kind of girl who couldn't concentrate on anything except her boyfriend (boyfriend??), but I was having serious trouble thinking about anything else. I sneaked a look at my phone. Exactly a week ago I'd been sitting with Joe in a beachfront cafe drinking coffee and putting the world to rights. A million miles away from a muggy classroom in Brighton.

Joe and I ended up spending hours together on the beach at the non-barbecue.

His friends eventually got bored of messing about in the sea and came to join us. I reluctantly sat up and straightened my skirt as they noisily went about getting drinks, putting down towels and dripping water on us. They smelled of boy: fresh sweat, beer and whatever they'd sprayed on that morning to make them fragrant. I shifted uncomfortably at the sudden change in dynamic.

Joe gestured airily in his friends' general direction and introduced them: 'Ben, Rav, Will: Sarah. Sarah: Ben, Rav, Will.'

I wasn't sure who was who, although I guessed that Rav was the one with the brown skin sitting in the middle. He smiled and said hello then immediately looked down at his hands. I relaxed slightly. We could be quiet and uncomfortable together.

'So, where you from, Sarah?' asked Ben/Will. He was short with a Scottish accent, but he could have been a local with his deep tan and dark-brown wavy hair. I put on my best first-impressions-count smile. 'Brighton. You?'

'Perth.' He lowered his voice. 'The one in Scotland.' I stared at him stupidly. 'As opposed to Australia?' I forced out a laugh, and he bowed slightly. 'I know, it's a shit joke. But thanks for laughing . . . Will's from Brighton, aren't you, Will?'

I started with the 'Oh really! Brighton! Wow, which bit!' stuff, but Will was monosyllabic all over. He was tall, broad and handsome in a ridiculous Hollywood way. All bronzed with cheekbones and flashing eyes. But he knew it, and he acted sort of tired and sardonic, like he didn't have to make an effort cos his smouldering good looks did the talking. Yawn. And his teeth were nowhere near as good as Joe's. As the conversation continued in its fairly agonizing, stilted way, I tried to be part of the conversation, but I was distracted by my conflicting emotions, and I couldn't concentrate. I was desperate for them to leave me and Joe alone again, but at the same time I didn't want them to in case Joe went with them.

In the end, Rav put me out of my misery. He announced he was starving so he, Ben and Will went off to get food. Joe told them he'd give it a miss. He wanted to stay with me. (He wanted to stay with me! I wanted a T-shirt with those words on it.)

As soon as the boys had sloped off, Joe fell back-wards on to the sand and stretched. 'Thank God for that. I thought they'd never leave.' He put his hands behind his head and grinned up at me. 'Thanks for sticking around.'

I smiled, and had just started the process of pluck-ing up enough courage to make the first move when he gently pulled me towards him. As we kissed, he stroked his hand up my leg, under my dress, up my thigh. I could feel my heart beating faster, partly cos it felt good, but a lot because of the scary new terri-tory. I gently pushed his hand away as it found its way under my knicker elastic.

'Don't you want to?' murmured Joe, kissing my earlobe.

I didn't know how to respond without breaking the mood, so I did a kind of kiss/shake-head/kiss manoeuvre while transferring his hand to my back.

Joe groaned, 'You're killing me, you know that?' and he kissed me hard, his tongue grappling with mine as he let out occasional little moans. It was horny as hell and I could have given up my virginity there and then if we hadn't been in public and I hadn't known him precisely twelve hours. I'm not a hopelessly unrealistic romantic, but I wanted more from such a momentous occasion than sand in my bits and a nagging worry that we could have provided someone walking by the beach with their own private porno. I'd already gone as far as I'd ever gone before.

So we carried on kissing (a lot) and talking (a bit), and that was more than enough for me. For now.

As the sky started to lighten, Joe and I lay on the sand, his arm round my shoulders and my head on his chest. I listened to his heart beating as bubbles of happiness burst inside me.

'I should get back,' I said finally, running my hand over the soft, washed-out cotton of his T-shirt and desperately not wanting the night to end.

He kissed the top of my head and said, 'Shame,' then reached down and murmured into my ear: 'I have plans for you, missy.'

Oh God. Lust lust.

'Yeah, well, you'll just have to lock them away,' I replied, clambering to my feet. It wasn't just my own mixed feelings about losing it that meant I needed to go. Assuming Joe wanted to take me back to wherever he was staying, I really didn't feel like trying to explain later to panicking parents exactly where I'd been. However, as I wasn't up for explaining the embarrassing parent factor to Joe either, I just said, 'Fancy meeting later?' I tried to sound offhand, in direct contradiction to my actual feelings.

Joe sat up and rested his elbows on his raised

knees. I tried not to stare at the sand caught in the fair hairs on his legs. 'Definitely.' He grinned and waggled his eyebrows saucily.

'At the cafe on the beach?' I said pointedly.

He gave me a little salute. 'Yes, of course. Sorry, Sarah Doesn't-like-beer.' And he suddenly jumped up and pulled me towards him by my waist. 'You are gorgeous,' he said, and went in for another deep kiss.

I managed to extricate myself, laughing as he pretended to grapple for me. 'Joe! I've got to go.'

He gave me a short sharp smack on the bum. 'Yes, go. And be at the cafe, four p.m., or there'll be trouble.'

'Quaking in my boots,' I mocked, then ran off giggling as he made a lunge for me. Amazing what some proper kissing can do for a girl's confidence.

I smiled all the way back along the winding shrub-lined path from the beach to our bungalow, breathing in the heady scent of lavender and juniper and feeling invincible. As the sun started to climb over the horizon, I quietly let myself in and locked the door behind me. Fortunately the place was silent save for a low electrical humming and the sound of the crickets outside. My flip-flops made a racket on the tiled floor, so I kicked them off and cautiously stuck my head round Mum and Dad's bedroom door to let them know I was back. Thankfully they didn't wake up enough to notice the daylight beginning to seep through their shutters. I went into the kitchen and opened the fridge. Ham, cheese, tomatoes, bread, chocolate. Perfect. I made a doorstep sandwich and put it on a tray, along with some crisps, a hefty slab of the chocolate and a glass of water and carried it through to the living room. I grabbed the remote and sat on the sofa, curling my legs under me. There were only Spanish TV channels, but I found an episode of *Friends*. Dubbed, of course, but still – it was kind of comforting.

Anyway, I didn't really want to watch TV. I just wanted to be. To be up as the sky lightened, eating the meal I'd missed because I'd spent hours on the beach kissing a beautiful, funny boy whose eyes made my heart flip.

I'd never even been close to feeling like this before. While I hadn't exactly been a late starter – I'd first got with a boy on a school trip to France in Year Eight – I'd never gone much further than kissing. That first time was on one of those activity holidays, and me and Cass had spent, like, two hours kissing two boys from another school. It was totally innocent, but I remember feeling really adult cos I was kissing like how grown-ups do it on TV. Sweet, no? But since then there hadn't been an awful lot of action. It wasn't cos I didn't want to; it was more that I didn't want to with any of the boys on offer. And so I became Sarah Millar: man-hater. Doesn't drink, doesn't flirt, doesn't put out. End of. The furthest I'd ever gone was being felt-up at a party in Year Eleven. (To be honest, I'd have gone further that time, but my dad arrived to pick me up. Tragic, yes, but it saved me from a potentially scary situation. Sam Massey, the boy in question, had an eighteenth-century-poet thing going on – all brown wavy hair, olive skin and soulful eyes. I'd always fancied him because, as well as being beautiful, he was a bit shy like me, and he talked to me like a human being. But he was also the boy who India Chadwick, the hardest girl in Year Ten, fancied. Stupidly, that was enough for me never to go there again. I spent a week afterwards ducking into doorways whenever I saw India, although amazingly she never found out I'd kissed her crush. Sam left after GCSEs to go to a different school. I don't know why. I still sometimes wondered what might have happened if India hadn't been in the way.)

And now there was Joe. Who I did really like. *Really* like. And who, incredibly, seemed to like me back. I sighed with contentment and tucked into my sandwich, while on the TV Ross and Rachel got it on.

4

My art-history teacher collared me at the end of the lesson to talk coursework so I was late getting to the canteen at lunchtime to meet the others. I looked over the sea of students and spotted Donna instantly. Hard not to, since she was standing on her chair waving like she was directing planes. I grabbed a cheese toastie and a Ribena, paid and hurried over.

'About time,' said Ashley, grabbing her bag off the one empty seat. 'Donna almost got into fisticuffs guarding this for you.'

'Sorry, sorry, Andrea kept me back,' I said, squeezing myself into the chair and stashing my bag underneath.

'Bloody hell, Sarah, in trouble already? The term's only just begun,' said Ash, putting her hand to her chest, shock-horror style.

'Ha ha.' I looked at my toastie and the greasy globs of orange cheese dripping on to my plate.

'You going to eat that?' asked Donna, her mouth full of chips.

I handed it over. 'No, you have it. I'm full.'

Cass frowned. 'Full? You haven't eaten a thing!'

Cass gets suspicious if she thinks one of us is dieting – that's her domain. She's got a gorgeous figure, but Adam likes skinny girls. And if that makes him sound like a knob that'll be because he's a knob. Anyway, despite the fact that Adam would never fancy one of us and we'd – ugh – never fancy him, for some reason Cass likes to be the thinnest. Go figure.

Ashley smirked into her Müller Light.

'What's so funny?' demanded Cass, her forehead creasing prettily. (Did I mention our Cassie is also super-sensitive about her Adam-based foibles?)

'Nothing,' replied Ash, taking spoonfuls of yogurt then turning them over so they dolloped back into the pot. 'Just Sarah losing her appetite over a boy.'

I gave her a look. 'Sorry to disappoint, but I had a Ripple, like, half an hour ago.' (A lie. I'd had no appetite since getting back from holiday. I wasn't about to admit it, though – it was pathetic to fancy a boy so much you couldn't even eat.)

'Anyway,' said Cass, 'kissing on the beach . . .'

'Yeah,' said Donna. 'Did you have dutty sex among the sand dunes?'

I shot lazy eyes in her direction. 'What do you think?'

Cass reached across the table to put her hand on mine. 'So go on, Sar. What did happen?'

The girls may as well have been invisible. I was right back there, the hot dusty smell of the holiday home and 'Sex on Fire', my not-purposely-ironic soundtrack to getting ready for Joe.

But that was later.

After meeting at the cafe, me and him spent pretty much every waking moment together. We walked around the town, tried out all the bars and cafes, sat on the beach and generally got to know each other. I learned that he's doing politics at uni in London, that he's got two sisters, that his parents are divorced but still friends, and that he really wants to work for Aids charities in Africa when he graduates cos his uncle died of Aids in the 1980s. I told him stuff I had only ever told a few people, like how my mum was married to a different man when she met my dad, and how I was bullied at primary school. He was a good listener, and he asked questions as though he really wanted to know the answer.

When we weren't talking, we kissed. But we didn't go much further than kissing. Frustratingly, every time we were at his place at least one of his friends was around, and not only was it a tiny holiday chalet, but he and Will shared a room. One time we were kissing on Joe's bed – dressed, but only just – when Will marched in, saw us, said, 'Oops, sorry,' and marched out again. But I was mortified. I buried my face in Joe's neck and groaned. 'So. Embarrassing.'

He laughed. 'What's the big deal?' He tried to push me off him so he could see me, but I wouldn't let him. 'Sarah, c'mon. He doesn't care, honestly.' He caressed my bum through my denim shorts then slipped his hand under the waistband. 'At least we know he'll leave us alone now . . .'

I sat up and moved to the edge of the bed. 'No way!' I waited a moment for the burning in my face to subside, then offered my hand to pull him up. 'Come on, we have to go and show him we're not doing anything.'

Joe looked genuinely confused. 'But why?'

Obviously I hadn't told him I was a virgin. Why would I?

'Because I would die of embarrassment if I thought he thought we were doing . . . anything in his bedroom!'

'But it's my bedroom too,' said Joe.

I gave him a *that's not the point* look and wheedled, 'Pleeeease, Joe. Let's go for a drink or something . . . Please?' I smiled and batted my eyelashes, and he let me pull him off the bed.

Then an opportunity arose. Mum and Dad wanted to take me and Dan out for dinner. I hatched a plan to mope around all afternoon clutching my midriff then cry off at the last minute, pleading period pains.

Joe immediately agreed to come round. I knew what he would think the invitation meant. And I was pretty sure it meant that too. Believe me, I had thought long and hard about it. But my shaved legs, best knickers and condoms from the machine in the cafe toilets spoke for themselves. I was pretty sure tonight was the night. But, still, I planned to wait and see how I felt when Joe arrived.

Two hours later, I was no longer a virgin.

'SHUDDUP!' screamed Donna, smacking her hand on the table and sending the condiments flying. 'You so can't leave it there!'

'Yeah, c'mon, hon,' said Cass, her knees bouncing like pistons. 'What was it like?'

'And details please,' added Ashley, making a most unladylike gesture.

'All right, ask me anything you like,' I said, holding out my hands. 'I am an open book.'

Ash leant forward in her seat. 'OK. Did he have a big dick?'

'Dunno,' I said, looking around to check no one was earwigging. 'Don't have anything to compare it to.' (Although, to be honest, it had seemed alarmingly huge. Let's just say it was bigger than any tampon.)

Cass shot Ashley a scornful look. 'You're obsessed

with willies.' She turned to me and smiled indulgently. 'Was it romantic?'

I sighed. 'Totally. We had a real connection. It felt . . . inevitable. Like a chain reaction or something. Like, we were kissing, then his hand was up my top, then inside my skirt, then I put my hand on his willy through his shorts . . .'

Whoops and a round of applause from Donna and Ash at this point. So mature, those two. I rolled my eyes at them, although if I'm honest I was loving having a sex story to tell at last.

'Anyway. It sort of went from there. We didn't really talk. I knew I wanted it to happen, so I just went with it and it kind of . . . happened. Know what I mean?'

'Totally,' said the girls in unison.

It really had felt inevitable. As soon as he walked through the door we were kissing, just standing there drinking each other in. I closed my eyes and let him stroke my hair away from my face, then he gently pulled away and smiled at me. I held out my hand and he took it, and I led him in the direction of my bedroom. There was no need to say anything – I know, it's a cliché, but it was totally like we were on the same wavelength. It took about ten minutes to get to the bedroom, as he kept stopping to kiss me, pushing me against the wall and running his hands down my arms. By the time we reached my room I couldn't have held back if you'd paid me. Thank God I'd picked up those condoms, although to be fair Joe produced one too. We could have done it four times, we were that well provided for in the contraceptive department.

But we just did it the once. He left about five minutes afterwards. I guess he was right: my parents could have got back at any time.

I didn't tell the girls everything. It hadn't been amazing. I mean, it had been nice, but to start with it had hurt, a bit, and I didn't make noises or anything. The earth didn't move. You know what I'm saying.

But that didn't bother me.

What bothered me was that the next day he went back to England. We had to say goodbye in front of everyone else who was leaving that day. About thirty people milled around the coach that the holiday company had provided to take them to the airport, its engine idling away in the heat. It wasn't exactly romantic. Obviously we hugged, and kissed – an amazing, soft, tender kiss that makes my lips tingle every time I think of it (which is a lot) – and Joe leant down and whispered, 'I'll miss you,' into my ear, which made me cry despite all my efforts, but I wished we were alone. He wiped a tear away with his thumb, smiled this sad little smile and said, 'I'll call you soon.' And then he was on the coach and I was crying properly as he craned his neck to keep waving at me.

I hadn't heard from him since.

And he had taken up permanent residence in my brain. I could not stop thinking about him. I just had to be patient: he'd promised to call, so he'd call. But, AAGH, the waiting was killing me.

'Oh, mate, that sucks,' said Donna, looking genuinely sympathetic, while Cass squeezed my hand and Ashley shook her head in disgust at Joe's failure to keep his promise.

'Thanks, but I'm fine, honestly!' I said, although my mood had plummeted ten shades darker. 'He didn't say *when* he'd phone. And I've only been back a couple of days.'

'Why don't you call him then?' asked Ash.

I shrugged sheepishly. 'I don't have his number.'

Donna slapped her forehead. 'Shit, Sarah! Boys always refuse to give you their number if they're only up for no-strings pulling. It's like a boy law or something.'

'It wasn't like that,' I said, my face beginning to burn. 'It's not that he refused to give me his number, just that he asked for mine, so I didn't think . . . Look, you can believe what you want, but I was there and I'm telling you. It was special.'

Cass shot Donna a warning look before turning wide eyes to me. 'Course it was, honey. You wouldn't give it up for anyone.'

'Exactly.' My vision went blurry as my eyes filled with tears. I pretended to look for something in my bag. Didn't fool the girls for a second, of course, but they were sweet enough to pretend. I didn't know whether I was crying cos Joe hadn't been in touch or because Donna, and probably Ashley, thought he was a wanker. I sneaked a look at Cass, who was staring at me with concern. I didn't want to be like her: besotted with an unfaithful idiot who all your friends know is an unfaithful idiot.

'Look, if it really did mean as much as you say – which I'm sure it did,' Ashley held up her hand to stop any protest, 'then maybe, I dunno, he lost his phone or something.'

I sniffed. 'Yeah. I did think that could be it.'

Cass patted my knee. 'Well, there you go, hon. You write to him care of his uni, he gets back to you, and all is well.'

Donna gaped at Cass like she'd just suggested I send myself as a naked telegram. 'Yeah, right. And what if he just hasn't got round to calling her?' She turned to me. 'You writing him a letter is just going to

34

tell him you're a stalker. If you must go down that route, work out his uni email address and contact him that way.'

Ashley butted in: 'But only if you have a reason. Don't just email saying, "Hi! It's me! Why haven't you called?" like some mental bunny boiler. Say you're going to be in London visiting a friend or something, and if he happens to be around you thought it'd be nice to catch up.'

I mused on that one for a moment, little prickles of hope stirring in my gut. 'And he definitely won't think that's stalkerish?'

'He might,' shrugged Ash. 'That's the risk you take.'

Donna nodded. 'Yeah, actually I'd leave it a bit longer. Wait another, like, two weeks. After that you've got nothing to lose by contacting him.'

I looked at Cass to see what she thought, but she pretended to be engrossed in her tuna salad. Which probably meant she disagreed with the other two.

Brilliant. I might be an A-grade student, but I'm a total failure when it comes to the opposite sex. I felt a stab of annoyance. Bloody Joe, being all sexy and attentive and invading my every thought then disappearing into the ether. I tried to ignore the ache in my loins and resolved to give him exactly fourteen days. If he hadn't been in touch by then, I was sending him an email. I didn't care what Donna and Ashley said. Anyway, they always agreed with each other – you could pretty much count them as one person.

'Anyway, look on the bright side,' said Donna, rocking back on her chair. 'We're Year Thirteens now – and there's only, like, ten months until we're officially released into the big, wide world . . . And soon we won't even need fake ID – BECAUSE IT'LL BE REAL!' She folded her arms and beamed around at us.

'Totally,' said Cass, sighing contentedly. 'And it's Jack's eighteenth next week.' She pointed her fork at me. 'See: something to look forward to already.'

Hmm.

Our mate Jack's parents had booked out the top floor of a pub for his birthday party. It was a full-on do, complete with 'Happy 18th Birthday' banner, grandparents, great-aunts downing white-wine spritzers and uncles sipping bitter and tapping their feet to the jolly young people's music, a finger buffet and a huge cake in the shape of a football shirt with 'Jack is' written across the top and '18' in the middle. (Jack's a proper sports whizz. If we lived in America he'd wear one of those red-and-white jackets with the letters on the back and be dating a cheerleader. As it is he owns enough polyester sportswear to burn Brighton to the ground, he's a lifeguard at our local pool at weekends and doesn't have a girlfriend. Not that he doesn't have his fair share of WAG wannabes – he is, after all, a fit blond footballer. He's just a bit like me, I suppose: discerning.)

Jack's mum had asked me, Cass, Ashley, Donna and our other friends Rich – Jack's best mate – and Ollie to help blow up balloons, set out the buffet and generally get the place looking like her idea of a dream party venue. Which is to say not exactly *our* idea of a dream party venue, although to be fair Jack would have loved it whatever she did. If he ever makes it big he'll make a rubbish celebrity footballer. He's far too nice and sensible.

We put the last plate of pineapple and cheese on sticks on the table, symmetrically placed between a pile of napkins and a stack of paper plates, while Jack's mum stood in the middle of the room, hands on hips. 'It's great,' she sighed. 'Well done, everyone.'

Ash caught my eye and gave me an *aw, bless* look. Jack's mum was so welling up. I suppose it's a big thing when your only child turns eighteen.

I sneakily checked my phone. Still no messages. There were only a few days left till Joe's deadline, and I wasn't having any luck emailing him. (My plan had changed slightly, in that I'd decided to try emailing straight away while giving him a two-week deadline to get in touch. Kind of nearly the same as plan A, but with the added bonus of pandering to my total lack of willpower.) Every possible permutation of his name and his uni's web address bounced back. But I wasn't going to think about that tonight. The DJ had just arrived, and he was wearing an actual powder-blue tux over an actual cream ruffled shirt. If anything was going to take my mind off Joe, it was a comedy DJ who didn't realize he was comedy.

While DJ Cheese was setting up, the birthday boy arrived. He sidled in, looking uncomfortable at being the star of the show. So of course we cheered and leapt on him in a birthday bundle before breaking into an impromptu rendition of 'Happy Birthday To You', complete with harmonies. Rude not to.

'Thanks for that, guys,' said Jack, smiling and straightening his shirt. 'You going to give me the bumps next?'

'Don't tempt us,' said Rich, handing Jack a drink. 'Happy birthday, mate.'

Cass did little lady jumps and clapped her hands. 'Adam's waiting outside, so, quick, give him his prezzie, give him his prezzie!'

Rich ran back to our table and fetched a gift bag from where he'd hidden it under his coat. 'Carefully wrapped by *moi*,' he said, handing it over while we all stood jittering with present-giving trepidation.

'Aw, thanks, guys.' Jack reached into the bag and pulled out an original programme from the 1982–83 FA Cup Final between Brighton & Hove Albion and Manchester United. Rich had won it on eBay for £30, and we'd all contributed.

Jack's face broke into an enormous grin. 'Shit, that's awesome!' He laughed with delight and flicked the pages. 'Man. It's brilliant . . . Seriously, thanks so much.'

Rich thumped him on the back. 'You're welcome.'

It was lovely. Even miserable me couldn't help smiling at how much Jack loved our present. Then a squeal of feedback announced that the DJ was about to start his set, and the moment was broken. Cass ran off to fetch her man and the rest of us gawped at DJ Blue Tux.

'Evening, pop-pickers – I'm Alan and I'll be spinning the platters that matter to celebrate Jaaaack's eighteenth birthdaaaaay! So let's start as we mean to go on . . . with a funky slice of puuuure disco. Iiiiit's . . .' [dramatic pause] 'the Bee Geeeees!'

By this point the girls and I were falling all over each other in joy. 'Oh my God, I LOVE this man. I want to HAVE HIS BABIES!' whooped Ashley, dropping to her knees in ecstasy.

Donna stood up and straightened her top in a businesslike manner. 'I'm so going to make a request.'

And we all trotted after her as she marched over to Alan, who was biting his bottom lip and getting funky to 'Stayin' Alive'. She pulled his sleeve and he turned to us, taking his headphones off one ear and smiling expectantly.

'Are you doing requests?' she asked.

'Not yet, but I will be later when the olds are a bit drunker. First half's for them, innit. Gives everyone a good time.'

And our mouths all fell open like someone had put a coin in a slot, because when Alan spoke he was broad Sarf London and, underneath the suit and guy-liner, he was actually not that much older than us.

Ashley narrowed her eyes. 'Are you really called Alan?'

He smiled. 'I am tonight.'

'Oh go on, tell us your real name,' wheedled Donna, but he just shook his head. I saw Ashley quietly appraising him. I so knew what was going through her mind.

The song came to an end and 'Alan' nodded cordially at us. Translation: *Nice to meet you, but go away now.*

'Ash, tell me you're not going to pull the DJ,' I said when we'd got back to our table.

She tossed her hair. 'Why not? Bet he'd tell me his real name.'

I shook my head sorrowfully. 'Where's the romance in your soul?'

She stuffed a mushroom vol-au-vent in her mouth. 'Don't have any.' She waggled her fingers at me. 'Got fire in my loins instead.' Or I think that's what she said.

'Oh God, it's him.' Donna scowled in the direction of Cass and her boyfriend, who had just arrived and were walking towards us hand in hand, Cass leaning into him like walking had become a bit of a stretch. Adam had that effect on her. She seemed to regress fifteen years when they were together. She even stood differently, with her toes turned in. Maybe it was because he was older than her, or knew her parents, or something. He was twenty-one and worked for Cass's dad's building company. He'd got the job straight from school because Cass's dad knew his dad and he was friends with Cass's brother, or something. It was all a bit icky and incestuous, anyway. He and Cass had met when she was fourteen and doing some office adminy-type work for her dad over the summer. Adam was insanely good-looking and could totally turn on the charm when he wanted to, and her parents thought the sun shined out of his arse: let's just say there was never any issue about Adam sharing Cass's bedroom. It was really infuriating, cos you just knew that they'd go mental if they found out what he was really like.

Anyway, he totally had Cass under his spell, and she turned into an annoying person when they were together. She knew it, too, but she was too much in love with him to do anything about it. Hey ho.

'Hi, everyone,' sang Cass, giving us a little wave. 'Go and get the drinks, will you, babe?' she asked Adam, leaning up to kiss him then wiping the lip-gloss mark off his mouth with her thumb. 'Usual for me.' He gave us a cursory glance and went off to the bar.

Cass sat down. 'Your mum rounded up the whole family, then?' She smiled, looking around the room. The tables were rapidly filling up, mostly with complete strangers. Jack looked slightly embarrassed.

'Yeah. And the rest.' His mum was from a big family so Jack had like a million cousins, and she pretty much knew everyone because of her charity and outreach-type work. His dad, on the other hand, did some kind of local government work and barely spoke. He could have been a professional assassin for all I knew. He took keeping himself to himself to a whole new level.

'Well, I think it's lovely,' said Cass, stroking his arm. 'And I bet you a million pounds the DJ is three songs minimum away from playing the Grease Megamix, which everyone knows is when a good party becomes an AWESOME party.' Ash raised an eyebrow but said nothing. She can be a bit earnest when it comes to music, although give her a few drinks and she'll leap about to 'I Will Survive' like the best of us.

Suddenly Rich pressed himself against me. 'Ooh, Sarah, your pocket just vibrated.'

I gave him a shove, 'Gerroff, perv.' But I wasn't offended. Rich is the loveliest guy on the planet. And not into girls. Not that you'd know it if you didn't know it, if you know what I mean.

'Well?' asked Donna, as I checked my phone.

I shook my head. 'It's from my mum.' It wasn't anything that couldn't have waited till she saw me. I put my phone away and waited for the adrenalin rush to subside. Talk about hope springs eternal. Every time my phone rang, I hoped it was Joe. I even *expected* it to be Joe, which was just stupid.

Ollie stood up. 'C'mon, then. Who's dancing?' And he shimmied on to the square of scuffed wood in front of DJ Alan's booth, hunching his shoulders and pointing his fingers like a badass. He was the only (straight) boy I knew who'd happily be the first on the dance floor. How he managed to be the playboy of Woodside High, I do not know.

A couple of middle-aged women were doing the step-slide-step to 'Don't Stop Believin'', and Ollie gleefully joined them. He knew all the words too.

Donna and I pushed our chairs back and stood up as one. 'Anyone else?' I asked, but the rest of the table declined. Cass usually loves a dance, but not when Adam's around. So me and Donna boogied over to Ollie, and there we stayed for a good five songs. It was brilliant, and the first time I hadn't thought about Joe since I'd left him in Spain.

'Wahey, Aerosmith!' Rich suddenly appeared beside us, twanging away on his air guitar and head-banging like a crazy person. Donna narrowed her eyes.

'Rich . . . ?'

He looked confused and then, getting her meaning, shook his head vehemently. 'No, course not.' He looked hurt. 'In front of my best mate's family? C'mon . . .' Rich was a bit of a one for the illegal sub-stances, but it was another thing about him you wouldn't know unless you knew. Dancing until the sweat poured out of him was usually a sure sign, although tonight it seemed he was just on a natural high.

'I'm parched,' announced Donna when we got back to the table. She grabbed the water jug. 'I'll get a refill.'

'Cass, what's going on?' asked Ollie, sitting beside her. 'Grease Megamix wasn't the same without you. I did the man bits and everything.' Cass just shrugged and smiled unhappily. Weird. Ollie and I exchanged confused looks.

'Actually, I think I'll get a drink too,' she said. 'Same again, babe?' Adam caressed her bum as she stood up, which was apparently code for 'Yes please'. Jack put down the remains of a giant scotch egg he'd manfully been working his way through.

'I'll come with you. S'pose I should say hello to people.'

Adam coughed. 'Don't think so, mate . . . Sit down, babe. I'll get the drinks.' He gestured for Jack to go first then followed him with his usual cacked-my-pants swagger.

'Uh, what was that?' asked Donna.

Cass looked miserable. 'Adam's got a bee in his bonnet about Jack again. He saw me "touch him" earlier, or something.' She ran her hand through her hair. 'It's so silly.'

Silly was one word for it. 'Babes, you've got to sort this out,' said Donna. 'It's not like you can change the fact you and Jack have known each other forever. How many times have you told Adam there's never been anything between you?'

'I know. He's just a bit insecure,' said Cass. 'He'll get over it eventually.' But she didn't look convinced.

At that moment the object of Cass's blind adoration

appeared back at the table, empty-handed. We all immediately and very obviously stopped talking, but he didn't seem to notice. He took Cass's coat off the back of her chair and held it out.

'Actually, babe, let's go. This party's lame.'

And without a murmur she put her arms into her coat.

'Bye then,' said Ash, pointedly. Cass turned back for a moment, smiled apologetically and mouthed, *Sorry*, then trotted obediently after him, but a few seconds later she was back. 'He's just gone to the loo. Tell Jack I'm really sorry for leaving early, will you?' Before we had time to respond, she'd rushed off again.

Two hours later, Ash was sucking the face off some cousin of Jack's, obviously having decided to give DJ Alan a miss; Ollie had hooked up with Jas Mistry, a girl in the year below us, and was nowhere to be seen; Donna, Rich and Jack were doing shots; and I was moping. I wasn't drunk enough to find the boys and Donna as hilarious as they found each other, and I missed Joe. I was sick of my heart leaping every time my phone made any kind of noise, only to have it break a tiny bit because it wasn't him. But I wasn't quite ready to admit defeat. After all, he had a few days left before his deadline was up. Not that he knew that.

I heaved a hefty sigh. Fun as it was watching Donna, Jack and Rich getting very drunk, I'd had enough. 'I'm going to make a move,' I announced, but they weren't listening. So I left.

On Joe's deadline day I kept my phone glued to my hand. There was almost some cosmic rightness in him getting back to me today, just as I'd nearly given up hope. Like a test of my commitment, or something. I know: mental. But I couldn't believe that the connection we'd had didn't mean anything. So even as the day came to an end, I remained optimistic. I was almost certain he'd get in touch.

Then as we were leaving school Donna asked me if I'd heard anything.

'No, but –'

She interrupted: 'God, men are dicks.' She gave me a hug. 'You gave him every chance, babes . . . Put this one down to experience.' As I watched her walk away towards her bus stop, I finally realized it. He was never going to phone me. I'd given up my virginity to a holiday romance. I told myself it didn't matter. Being a virgin wasn't anything to be proud, or not proud of. It just was.

But it did matter. It mattered a lot. I had really, really liked him. Still did.

I tried anger on for size, aka the Donna and Ashley

way, but it didn't fit. I wasn't angry with Joe; I was angry with myself for being so bloody gullible.

Then came self-deprecation. 'Ha ha, typical! I'm such a doof! Durr!' *slaps forehead* But that was wrong too.

So in the end I settled for plain old weeping. Into my pillow, on to Cass's shoulder, and once, embarrassingly, right in the middle of French. Ollie covered for me, earnestly telling our teacher Monique that he'd told me such an amazing joke I was actually crying with laughter, which made me snort a snot bubble.

It was a horrible time.

But then I got the text.

5

It was the Friday night after the Monday of the two-week deadline, and we were in The Hobbit: me, Donna and Ashley, Cass, Rich and Jack, and Ollie. And, unfortunately, Adam. He had Cass on his knee, the better to whisper in her ear, in response to which she'd giggle and give him a lily-livered slap. God, it was annoying.

I was so not in the mood. But the whole night had been organized by the boys as a cheer-up-Sarah event, so I couldn't cry off to partake in my new hobby, the three Ms of getting over Joe: music channels (extra points for crying at cheesy ballads), microwave chips and moping.

So I'd put on clean jeans and one of my dad's shirts, given my eyelashes a couple of half-hearted flicks with the mascara brush, dutifully turned up on time and, as always, was the first one there. I'd parked myself at one of the picnic tables outside, the weather being stupidly warm for late September, and hunched over my watermelon Bacardi Breezer (I only like alcohol if it doesn't taste of alcohol).

Usually I loved this table, with the fairy lights in the trees casting everything in a blue glow and the noise from inside reduced to an atmospheric buzz, but all I could think about was my PJs and my bed. And Joe, obviously. He was still rudely trespassing all over my thoughts, with his lovely clean toenails and shapely calves. I growled and shook my head to get rid of the image, handily scaring away a couple of Emos who were about to share my table.

'Hairy McSarey!' came a voice from behind me. Ollie plonked down next to me, planted a kiss on my cheek and ruffled my hair. From anyone else it would have been irritating.

'Hey,' I said, forcing a smile.

'Others not here yet?' he asked.

I took a breath. Right. Socializing. 'Nope.' I looked around. 'I thought you were coming with Rich and Jack.'

Ollie drummed two fingers on the table, his knees banging a counterpoint underneath. He's always been a fidget. In primary school he was forever getting told off for playing with other kids' hair during carpet time. Maybe that's why he's so into music now – playing the guitar and stuff seems to help channel all that nervous energy.

'The others are at the bar,' he said, closing his eyes and biting his lip in funky concentration as whatever music was playing in his head reached a crescendo.

'So,' he said suddenly, opening his eyes and putting away the imaginary finger drum kit, 'How's the heartache?'

I picked at the label on my bottle. 'Oh. You know. Still there.'

He put his arm round my shoulder and did a hearty man-squeeze. 'Well, you can forget all about it tonight.'

I managed a weak smile. He meant well, but Ollie had no idea what I was going through, a one-night stand being a bit too much of a commitment for him.

'Here they are,' he said, waving Rich and Jack over just as Donna and Ashley appeared, glued to each other as always. Five minutes later, Cass and Adam turned up and our little party was complete.

Calloo and indeed callay.

When my phone vibrated I could hardly summon the energy to pick it up.

'Hey, Sarah, you OK?' frowned Cass, as I opened the text and the colour drained from my face.

Was I OK? I looked up, a huge smile making my lips crack; it'd been so long. The girls' eyes widened to Bratz proportions.

'No frickin' way!' shouted Donna, grabbing for my phone. I pulled it out of her reach. Cass squealed and did a spot of super-fast girl-clapping. Even Ash was grinning.

'What?' said Jack, looking confused. Rich and Ollie looked just as vacant. Poor remedial boys.

Ashley stuck her tongue into her bottom lip. 'Duh! She's got a text from Joe.'

'Oh shit. Nice one. What does it say?' asked Jack, trying to seem interested, bless him.

I opened the text again and held my phone up so the others could read it. They all hunched forward.

> Hi sarah. Am back at uni.
> Must see u! Come this
> weekend? Joe xx

Cass squealed again. 'Oh my God, you have to go!'

I bit my lip. 'Really? It won't make me seem, like, easy?'

Ashley put a fingertip on her chin and cocked her head to one side. 'Hmm, let me think.' I rolled my eyes at her. 'No, he won't think you're "easy",' she continued, making speech marks in the air, 'because we aren't actually living in the nineteen fifties.'

'Yeah, loosen up, lady,' said Donna. She pointed her beer bottle at me. 'You want him?' I gave her a look. 'Go get him then! Shit, it's not rocket science.'

Well, when she put it that way.

I started to text a reply.

'Whoa, what are you doing?' demanded Ollie, whipping my phone out of my hand.

'Yeah, you can't reply *now*,' added Rich. 'He kept you waiting.'

I looked around the table. Everyone was in agreement, it seemed. Even Adam was nodding sagely. I sighed. 'Sorry, guys. I'm not into playing games. I always reply to texts straight away. Right?' Acknowledgement all round. 'So, if you'll excuse me, I have an invitation to accept.' I held my hand out for my phone then turned my back on everyone with a flourish.

I could imagine the *ooh get her* looks my friends were exchanging, but I was too excited to care. He'd replied! He, quote, had to see me! Yes, he'd taken nearly three weeks to get in touch, but he'd probably just been busy. Loads to organize before going back to uni, etc. And patience had never been my strong point. I quickly typed:

> Yep why not. I'll get train
> to Victoria tomoz AM. Text
> me details! Sx

Talk about emotional rollercoaster. I was high on joy – and feeling like a tiny bit of an idiot for having played the drama queen. I hugged myself with glee and got on with enjoying myself, putting to the back of my mind the small matter of telling my parents that I was going to spend the weekend with Joe.

*

I didn't get home till gone midnight, so it was morning before I had a chance to talk to Mum and Dad. I was showered, dressed and at the table eating my Alpen when Mum came downstairs.

'I thought I heard you up and about,' she said, planting a kiss on the top of my head. 'Tea?'

I grunted assent through a mouthful of muesli mulch. She busied herself with kettle, mugs and teabags for a couple of minutes. 'So. How are you feeling?' she finally asked casually. I rolled my eyes. She was desperate for me to stop moping.

'Yeah, good actually,' I said brightly.

Mum beamed like I'd given her a present. 'Excellent! About time you snapped out of the post-holiday malaise.'

'Yeah, well. I'm fine. Thanks.' I loved my mum, but she could grate on my nerves like a knife squeaking against a plate.

She gave me another kiss before putting my tea down in front of me. 'Well, I'm pleased . . . So. Any plans for the weekend?'

I was pretty sure she would not be impressed if I told her I was skipping up to London for a weekend love-in. So I lied.

'Ash's mum's away so she's having the girls over for a DVD and pizza weekend.' I made a show of looking at the time on the microwave. 'I'll be off in a minute, actually.'

I was pretty proud of this little deception. It was wholesome enough for Mum to approve, but the fact that she's not a huge fan of Ashley's would ensure she didn't instantly think I was making it up. Although actually she'd probably have believed whatever I told her. I'd never lied to her or Dad like this before.

'At nine o'clock in the morning? That's a lot of DVDs.'

I got up to put my bowl in the dishwasher. I didn't trust my face not to give me away. 'We're spending the day at the beach first. Making the most of this Indian summer.' I nodded towards the window. Which was covered with a fine mist of drizzle. Huh. Maybe should have thought that one through.

Still, Mum accepted it. I felt bad for deceiving her, but she wanted to believe I was having fun. And, anyway, my excitement at the thought of seeing Joe outweighed my guilt by about seventeen billion to one.

I skipped upstairs to grab my bag with a song in my heart and a salsa rhythm in my rudey bits. I had a quick look in the mirror on the landing and beamed at my reflection. Joe Joe Joey Joe! I checked the time on my phone. In three hours, we'd be together.

*

But as the train sped through the stations my giddiness gave way to nerves. I'd been so caught up in the joy of Joe I hadn't thought about the fact that it wouldn't just be him there but all his uni mates too.

I chewed my lip and stared at the countryside rolling by. Even the clothes I'd packed seemed wrong. Would all his friends be smoking spliffs and making intellectual jokes? And if the conversation got on to politics – or, let's face it, any kind of current affairs that didn't involve TV or celebs – I was screwed.

At Victoria I joined the mass of people filing through the ticket gates. I pulled my Tube map out of my pocket for the hundredth time. Joe had given me directions and I'd been to London loads, but this was the first time on my own. As soon as I was through the gates I found a space by a cash machine and stopped for a moment to gather myself. I closed my eyes and was halfway through a cleansing in-breath when right in front of me a voice said, 'This is no time for a nap.'

I almost died of shock. My eyes pinged open and, before my brain had engaged, I'd given Joe a shove. 'Bloody hell, you scared the shit out of me!'

He laughed, revealing those beautiful teeth, and pulled me to him for a proper, full-on, with-tongues pash. A little bit of me felt bad for indulging in such a major PDA. I hate people who get it on in public.

But this was different. It was our passionate reunion. I let my body fall into his. His hands and mouth were cold, his suede jacket was rough and warm, and he smelled delicious.

'God, it's good to see you,' said Joe into my hair. Then he grabbed my hand, picked up my bag and moved off in the direction of the Tube. 'C'mon,' he called over his shoulder. 'I'm going to splash out on a cab.'

Extravagant behaviour for a student, but hey – seemed Joe thought I was worth it. The thought made my head spin. I wrapped my happiness round me like a faux fur coat. I was so lucky.

We kissed all the way to Kensal Green, my leg thrown over Joe's and his hands entwined in my hair. At his house Joe threw the fare at the driver and practically dragged me through the front door and up the stairs.

Inside his room he stopped for a moment, holding my chin with his thumb and forefinger and smiling a slow, sexy smile. 'Sarah Doesn't-like-beer, I need you in my bed,' he whispered.

I knew what he meant. I needed him like breathing.

Hopping on each foot in turn, Joe pulled his shoes off, then undid his jeans and let them drop to the floor. I'd been staring agog, but the sight of the ridiculous bulge in his pants impelled me to action. As I kicked off my knickers I couldn't believe I was being so brazen. I hadn't been naked in front of anyone since I was about ten (I kept my skirt on that time in Spain. Dunno why – it's just how it happened). But I could hear Ashley's voice in my head telling me to just go with it. So I did.

Within seconds we were on Joe's bed and his hands were everywhere. Even though we'd done it before, I was still in no way sure what I was meant to do, so I just did what felt right.

But Joe. Oh my God. He knew what he was doing. He worked his way around my body until I was helpless and writhing beneath him. This was so much better than the first time.

It was like the two of us were at the centre of a whirlwind, with Joe's hands at the eye of the storm. The intensity built almost unbearably. And then he stopped.

He reached behind him to pull a condom from under his pillow.

And then we were moving together properly, like it's supposed to be. I grabbed his bum as he went faster and faster, his eyes shut tight and the muscles in his arms quivering.

He tensed and shouted out, and suddenly everything was quiet save for the sound of Joe's heavy breathing, beads of sweat forming on his forehead. The whole world seemed to slow down, like a spinning top coming to rest, and then he opened his eyes. I smiled at him. When we did it in Spain, I'd been worried if it had been OK for him, but this time I knew that it had. How could I not, after that? I was learning – we were learning together how this worked best for us.

'You are amazing,' he breathed, and he kissed me lightly on the lips before dropping on to the rumpled sheets beside me.

I lay silently while Joe dozed. The drizzle had cleared and the sun was bathing the room in its afternoon glow. I stretched my leg out from under the duvet and caught a shaft of light, wriggling my toes in the warmth. I looked around the room idly, taking in his posters (*Family Guy*, *Scarface*, *Avatar*), his desk with his laptop and a load of bits of paper, a cheap-looking chest of drawers with a telly on it. Your typical boy's room, I guessed.

'What time is it?' mumbled Joe.

I stroked his hair away from his forehead. 'I'll just have a look.' I got out of bed and padded across the carpet to get my phone from my bag, then hurried back to bed, snuggling in beside him. I pressed the button to bring the screen to life. 'It's nearly four.'

Joe stretched and yawned, then rolling on to his side he took my hand and placed it on his very erect penis. 'Plenty of time for round two, then.'

A few hours later, we dragged ourselves out of bed and, after showering off the sweat of the afternoon, got the Tube into central London.

'You look lovely,' Joe whispered in my ear as we sat next to each other on the train. I smiled at him.

'Thanks. You don't look too bad yourself.' He looked delicious, of course, in jeans and a John Lennon T-shirt. At the next stop a woman got on and stood in front of us, holding on to the overhead rail. I sneakily looked her up and down, admiring her skinny jeans, trench coat and trilby. Joe leant over again.

'What does she look like?' he said in a low voice. 'Men's hats on girls just look stupid. I mean, is she *trying* to look like a lesbian?' I didn't say anything, and we spent the rest of the journey in companionable silence, Joe stroking the inside of my hand with his finger.

And then it was lovely walking hand in hand through the crowds and the lights to the pub where we were meeting Joe's friends. *This could be our future*, I thought. Sharing a flat in London, going out at the weekends and always having a soft spot for this place because it's where we went during our first weekend together.

'Earth to Sarah,' said Joe, gently tapping my head.

I shook the fantasy away. 'Sorry . . . I was just thinking about tonight.' I looked up at him. 'D'you think your friends will like me?'

Joe squeezed my hand. 'Course they will. What's not to love?' (Love?!) He brought us to a stop. 'Here we are.' He let go of my hand to push open the door of a wide-fronted building and I followed him into a large, crowded bar – it wasn't particularly snazzy, but it wasn't the student dive I was expecting either. I trotted to keep up as he weaved through the tables into a back room, where from a corner near the pool table a girl waved us over. She was sitting with four others: two girls and two boys.

'Joey!' squealed Waving Girl, and she stood up and leant across the table to throw her arms round my man.

'All right, Mimi,' grinned Joe. 'Starting as we mean to go on, then?' He nodded at the half-drunk bottle of wine on the table.

Mimi (what kind of a name is that?) wagged her finger at him. 'We're not all alcoholics like you.'

Joe laughed politely then put his hand on my back. 'Everyone, this is Sarah.'

I plastered on a grin and said, 'Hi! Nice to meet

you,' then gave a little wave. And instantly regretted it as being both lame and stupid. Everyone said hello back, although I noticed all three girls giving me the quick up-and-down appraisal. I took a deep breath and sternly reminded myself that Joe liked me so there was no reason at all why they shouldn't too.

'I'll find you a chair,' said Joe, and he disappeared, leaving me standing like a lemon. The girls openly stared at me and Mimi caught my eye. She stretched her mouth into a horrible parody of a smile then immediately dropped it, her eyes dead. I fought the urge to run away.

Three vodka and Cokes later, I was kind of enjoying myself. Ben and Rav were there. I hadn't recognized them when we'd first arrived. I'd only ever seen them in swimming shorts. Turned out they were also Joe's housemates – they'd made themselves scarce earlier on to give me and Joe some space.

But the girls were a different matter. They pretty much ignored me, talking and laughing among themselves. Mimi had long honey-coloured hair, which she kept swishing around like she was in a bloody Pantene advert, and she obviously loved the way her orange-painted nails looked on the side of her wineglass cos she kept waving it around to emphasize what she was saying.

I couldn't help stealing glances at the girls. They were only a few years older than me, but there was something about them. They seemed so confident and relaxed. They made me feel like a kid who'd been allowed to stay up with the grown-ups for a special treat.

Joe drained his bottle for what must have been the fifth or sixth time. 'Right, my round again.'

'No, I'll get this one,' I said, praying that the twenty-pound note in my purse would cover it. I stood up and hitched my bag on to my shoulder, but Joe pulled me back down.

'No, I'll get them,' he insisted, and I swear I heard one of the girls – a pretty one with blonde hair in a sharp bob – make some remark about ID.

By the time Joe got back with the drinks the girls had joined in with the boys' conversation. It seemed Bob Girl was called Lara or Mara or something, and the other one – lip gloss and black spiky hair – was Rosie. The conversation moved on to uni gossip and I tuned out. The boys made the odd attempt to include me, but there was no point. I had nothing to bring. I looked around the room and tried not to look bored.

'Uh, Joe?' said Mimi suddenly, eyeing me coolly. 'Think it might be about time to take your little friend home? Looks like it's past her bedtime?'

Mortification. The girls laughed and even Rav and Ben sniggered into their pint glasses. I pretended not to have heard and waited for Joe to defend me. But instead he plonked his arm heavily across my shoulders and leant over to clink drinks with Mimi, dragging me forward awkwardly.

'Don't worry, Meems, she's got a note from her mum,' he said, snorting with laughter. 'Right, babe?' and he gave me a perfunctory squeeze before removing his arm so he could thump his chest and burp at the same time.

I somehow managed to dredge up a smile. 'Yeah. Special dispensation for tidying my room.' As retorts go, I was quite pleased with that one, but no one heard. They were either laughing at Joe's comment or had already gone back to their own conversations.

I took a slow breath and blinked to get rid of the tears pricking my eyes. *Don't look upset, just ignore it. Don't look upset, just ignore it.* I stole a glance at the others. Ben caught my eye. He gave me a slow wink and slightly raised his glass. I smiled at him gratefully, but it just made me feel more lonely. Dunno how it's possible to feel lonely in a crowded pub sitting next to a boy who's spent the best part of the day with one or more parts of his anatomy inside you, but there you go.

The next couple of hours went agonizingly slowly.

I almost did an air-punch when last orders were called, but it was another half an hour before we finally left, and then we just ambled along the streets, the girls lurching all over the place and the boys taking it in turns to shove each other into the road.

I pulled Joe's sleeve to get his attention. 'Where are we going?'

He looked at me with drunken unfocused eyes. I hate that. 'Dunno, babe,' he slurred. God, he was really pissed. And I so wasn't loving this 'babe' thing. I didn't mind it from my friends, but from Joe it sounded boorish. Like Adam.

I gave up and trotted along behind them. I thought about going back to Joe's, but I didn't have a key. Or know how to get there. Or know where we were.

Nice work, Sarah, I thought. *Empowering stuff.*

At one point we stopped at a kebab shop so everyone except me could spend approximately twenty-seven years choosing what to order. Then even slower progress was made, until eventually we passed Warren Street Tube station (no use to me: it was closed) and Rosie shouted, 'Hey, let's go to Henrik's!' So we took a detour to one of their uni's halls of residence, where another fun-packed hour was spent squashed into this Henrik's room, sitting on his bed while the girls tried to persuade him to come out. He was so obviously not up for it that I'd have felt sorry for him if I hadn't felt so sorry for myself. I spent the hour looking around and wondering what it'd be like to go to uni here.

It was gone four by the time we got home, having parted with the girls at the night-bus stop. I didn't even remember them saying goodbye. One minute they were there, the next they weren't. It was about the only good thing to happen that entire night. It didn't get any better, either. Me and Joe went into his bedroom and I turned around to close the door, literally sighing with relief that it was all over. When I turned back, he was comatose.

All I could do was brush my teeth, get into bed beside him and wonder what the hell I was doing there.

6

'Sarah . . . Hey, Sarah.'

I slowly opened my eyes. Joe was leaning up on his elbow, watching me. He ran a finger down my forehead and over my nose, bringing it to a stop on my lips. He leant forward and, removing his finger, kissed where it had been, then he put his finger back and traced round my mouth. 'Sorry. I had to wake you.' He fixed his eyes on mine. 'You are so beautiful.' He paused. 'I need you.' And he kissed me deeply and tenderly, his mouth soft and warm on mine.

Oh God. I knew I should still be angry, but he'd been drunk last night. No one's really themselves when they're drunk. *This is the way Ashley and Donna do it*, I told myself. *Just go with it.* Joe pulled away from me then, and slowly kissed his way across my breasts and over my belly button, until his face was level with my crotch. I fought the urge to stop him when he started to take off yesterday's knickers, but then I felt his tongue on me, and the world disappeared again. And this time he didn't stop until my whole

67

body fizzed and hummed, and I grabbed his hair and whimpered.

A couple of hours later, we came up for air. Joe wrapped the second condom of the morning in a tissue and dropped it on the floor then, after planting an affectionate kiss on my right nipple, flopped on to the bed and pulled me to him.

'So am I right in thinking you came a grand total of three times this morning, young Sarah?'

I turned on to my side so I could see his face. As I thought: smug. 'Pretty pleased with yourself, aren't you?' I said, smiling.

He inclined his head modestly. 'The facts speak for themselves . . . And you're welcome.'

I laughed and shook my head in mock disbelief. 'Pride comes before a fall, Joseph.'

'What does that even mean?' he said, feigned confusion furrowing his rather lovely brow. 'Like, what does falling over have to do with pride?'

I laughed then realized that he wasn't joking. Maybe a knowledge of the metaphorical nature of old granny sayings isn't a vital component of a politics degree, but still. Duh. Anyway, it made me feel slightly less petrified about seeing his friends again. If nothing else I could dazzle them with 'Too wrongs don't make a right' and 'A bird in the hand is worth two in the bush' (although to be honest I didn't have a clue what that one was about).

Joe turned away from me, taking my arm with him so I curved round his back. 'So,' he said, kissing my hand. 'I guess the question on everyone's lips is: how do I compare with the others?'

I tried to sound light and unbothered. 'What others?'

He spun round so he was facing me again. 'No way. You weren't a virgin?' I shrugged and smiled. 'Wow. Well, I have to say: you're a natural.'

I beamed. As compliments go, it was way up there. 'You don't mind, then?' I asked, and he gave me a *what do you take me for* look and flopped on to his back. We lay silent for a minute. I raked my fingers lightly up and down his chest.

'Mmm, that's nice,' he murmured, his eyes closed. I watched his mouth curve with contentment and felt a slight thrill that it was me who was making him feel like that.

No use kidding myself. Last night might as well never have happened.

'So when did you lose yours, then?' I asked, keeping my voice low so as not to destroy the mood.

Without opening his eyes, he said: 'Fifteen. Honey Jessop. We went out for two years in the end.' He paused as if reminiscing. 'She gave brilliant blow jobs.'

'You lost your virginity to someone called Honey?' I ignored the BJ comment-slash-subtle hint. I knew that giving him oral sex was probably the polite thing to do, since he'd done me the favour, but I was also pretty sure that, when it came to sex, the normal rules of etiquette needn't apply. Bottom (ha ha) line? I just wasn't ready to put his willy in my mouth.

He grinned, showing his beautiful teeth. 'What can I say? I went to a posh school.'

I sniffed haughtily. 'Well, if I may say so, Joe is a much more sensible name for one's first shag.'

He put his arm round me and drew me close. 'Couldn't agree more.' He kissed the top of my head and we fell silent, eventually falling asleep in each other's arms.

I woke to find Joe fresh from the shower, naked and towelling his hair. It was the first time I'd seen his penis anything other than excited. It looked kind of sluggy.

'Get up, lazy bones,' he said, chucking me the towel. 'I need food.' I grinned happily and jumped out of bed, flicking his bum with the towel on my way out of the door. 'You'll pay for that, missy,' he called after me.

I giggled. I certainly hoped so.

*

'So, who were those girls last night?' I asked casually, studying the cafe menu. In the shower I'd started thinking about them again. That Mimi made me uneasy.

Joe wrinkled his forehead. 'I told you. Friends from uni.' He put his menu back in its little wooden holder in the middle of the table. 'What are you having?'

'Uh, scrambled eggs on toast, I think. No, I mean, who *exactly* are they?' I smiled at him. 'I'm just interested.'

'Scrambled eggs?' Joe scoffed. 'No way. You need a full English after all that exertion in my bed.' I felt his bare foot working its way up my leg. I pushed it down.

'Joe! I will not have such behaviour!' I raised one eyebrow in what I hoped was a seductive fashion. He stuck his bottom lip out.

'Sorry, Miss.' Slouching in his chair, he grinned mischievously. 'Can I help it if you drive me wild with desire?'

Funnily enough, the friends conversation didn't happen after that. Turned out sex talk over breakfast is most diverting, although a bit of a bummer when you have a train to catch. I crossed my legs and wondered if I was doomed to be permanently horny now I was with Joe. He got up to leave. 'Right,' he said, chucking a couple of notes on the table. 'I'll walk you to the station.'

Back on the street we walked in silence, just enjoying being together. 'I've had an amazing weekend,' I said, leaning into him. 'I would say you could come to mine next, but . . .' I didn't need to spell out that my parents would probably prove to be a bit of a downer on the whole riotous sex thing.

Joe squeezed my hand briefly. 'Yeah, well. I'll text you or something, yeah?'

Or something? I swallowed hard and opened my mouth, although I had nothing to say. He stopped and turned to me. 'Look. Sarah.' Oh God, he'd made his voice all gentle and conciliatory. Even with my limited experience, I knew what that meant. 'You're gorgeous, and great in bed, but I don't want you getting the wrong idea . . . and thinking this is something it's not.'

'Well, what is it then?' I felt sick.

Joe shrugged. 'It's a bit of fun, isn't it?' He smiled at me encouragingly. 'You're still at school and I have uni and everything . . . It's not like either of us is looking for a relationship.'

Leaving him in Spain had nothing on this. At least then there was hope. I let go of Joe's hand. I'd forgiven him once. I wasn't going to do it again. Turning to leave, I quietly said, 'I don't know what I want. But

I did think maybe it was more than just sex.' And then I walked away. He started to say something, but he quickly gave up, and then I heard him turn round and start back the way we'd come. I put my bag on the floor and clenched my fists tightly, my nails gouging crescent moons in the palms of my hands. I stared at the pavement. It was covered with patches of ancient dried chewing gum.

'Bye then,' I whispered.

At the station I bought a magazine and a Coke and sat rigidly on the platform, staring into space. When the train arrived I calmly boarded and walked along until I found an empty carriage, then dropped into a seat, not caring that my bag was blocking the aisle, and howled. I buried my face in my hands. Oh God, the humiliation. And Joe. Oh, Joe. The thought of not seeing him again made me want to die. I hauled my bag on to my knee, grabbed my phone then chucked the bag back on to the floor. I scrolled to Cass in my Favourites. She answered almost immediately.

'Hey, Mrs Joe, how'd it go?' she purred.

'Cass,' I hiccuped. 'I've been such a stupid cow.'

'Oh, honey, what happened?' I heard the sound of a door closing: Cass shutting herself away so she could talk to me in private. I could imagine the exact look of concern on her face.

I pinched the top of my nose as if that would stop me dissolving. 'It was amazing. But then it wasn't. But then it was again. And we had amazing sex. But . . .' I burst into tears all over again. 'He doesn't want me.'

Cass gasped. 'Did he tell you that?'

I felt a stab of protectiveness. Even after everything, I wasn't ready to hate Joe. 'Oh, it's not his fault really,' I said, sniffing. 'I just read way too much into it.' I started crying again. 'Why can't I be more like Ashley and just . . . *shag*? Why does it have to mean so much to me?'

'Look, hon, Ash talks the talk but she's not immune. C'mon, you remember the way she was last Christmas when that Mike guy chucked her.'

I did. She'd tried to pretend she didn't care, but Cass had seen her crying in the stationery cupboard.

I took a wavering breath. 'I know. But I was way too clingy with Joe.' I stopped, almost too embarrassed to go on. 'I thought we were making love,' I whispered.

Even over the sound of the train I could hear Cass sighing. 'Oh, honey.'

'I know,' I said, sobbing. I lifted my feet up on to the seat and hugged my knees. 'I drove him away.'

'No you didn't, hon. He's just a man. That's what they're like.'

*

I spent the rest of the journey back to Brighton scrolling through every mournful track on my iPod and going over and over the previous forty-eight hours. Yes, Joe had been distant at the pub, but he'd been so attentive that morning. And so sincere. Was it really just to get me to have sex with him? And the sex had been special, I'd felt it. Why did he look so deeply into my eyes if he was just using me? Was it possible to fake all that? (*Well, duh*, said the voice of reason, making a long overdue appearance.)

With these riddles on repeat, I dozed off, waking with a jolt every time my phone pinged with a text or call from one of the girls. I put it on Silent and went back to sleep, only waking in Brighton when the people going to London started boarding the train.

I stumbled home, my mouth dry, my head aching, and a bag of stones in the pit of my stomach. I wanted to forget the last two days had ever happened.

Next morning found us all in our tutor room waiting for Paul – head of maths and the person lucky enough to be in charge of our pastoral care – to turn up, count us in, then rush off to kick some more number-crunching butt. Paul was OK, if you ignored the fact that he acted more like a hotshot businessman than a teacher and used phrases like 'think outside the box'. And he was never in the room for more than five minutes of our twenty-minute tutor periods, which left a full fifteen minutes (maths!) for us to gently ease ourselves into the day.

But I didn't want any gaps in today. I wanted today to be busy, with no time for thinking. Or talking. So while Ashley and Donna discussed the film they'd seen that weekend, and Rich and Jack had a strange boy conversation about Saturday's *Doctor Who*, I studied *Heat* magazine as if the size of some soap star's thighs was the most fascinating thing I'd ever read, and hoped I'd be left alone. And I was, until Ollie appeared at my shoulder.

"'2012: The Year of the Sugar Daddy",' he read aloud, making me jump. 'Oh riiight. So that's why you've gone for an older dude.' He started poking me with his elbow, nudge-nudge-wink-wink style. 'What have they got that us young'uns haven't?'

'Fuck off, Ollie,' I snapped, pushing his arm away.

That wiped the grin off his face. 'Sorry, flower. I take it the weekend didn't go to plan then?'

I turned back to *Heat*. 'Just leave it, OK?'

Silence. Now they'd be worried. I sighed and pushed the magazine away. 'Look, I'm just in a bit of a bad place at the moment. I'll get over it.' Donna had been silent beside me, but as soon as she opened her mouth to speak I interrupted. 'Can we just say you live and learn, and leave it at that?'

'Yeah, of course,' she said. 'But, Sar, no one thinks badly of you.'

I fiddled with a pen to try to distract myself from crying again. 'Yes you do,' I said, my voice wavering. 'You think I'm an idiot. And you're right.' Everyone started chorusing, *No we don't, Joe's the idiot, blah blah*. Suddenly I felt exhausted. I looked around at my friends. Cass with her big watery eyes, Ashley and Donna exchanging worried looks. Even the boys looked concerned. Jack was practically wringing his hands, bless him. I attempted a smile.

'Honestly, I'll be fine. No one's died, I got the wrong idea about Joe, that's all.' I scraped my chair back. 'I just need to get a grip. Tell Paul I've gone to the loo, will you?' And I walked out of the room, out of school, and home, where I kicked off my shoes and crawled into bed.

In my dream Joe was sitting at my desk in the English room. He turned and smiled at me as I walked towards him. 'Appearance and reality in *Jane Eyre*,' he said, winking, then leant towards me conspiratorially and whispered, 'The reality is us.' Then he disappeared.

When I woke up I opened my bedroom window wide. I wasn't big into making life decisions based on my dreams, but I'd have been an idiot to ignore that one. Joe hadn't realized how good we were together, that was all. It was totally understandable that he was scared. He was a student in London, I lived – with my parents – fifty miles away. I was seventeen, he was twenty. It still hurt like hell that he'd blown me off – every time I remembered him walking away from me it was like being stabbed in the chest. But some things are worth fighting for.

Feeling miserable but resolved, I went into the bathroom, peeled off my clothes and turned the shower as hot as it would go. I stood naked and shivering while I waited for it to heat up, then got in and let the water pelt me for half an hour, eco-misery no match for my own. I washed my hair, conditioned it, then flipped open a tube of posh exfoliating stuff I'd got for Christmas but never used, poured a huge blob into my hand and slapped it all over, rubbing it in till my skin hurt. Then I got out of the shower, stood in the fragrant fug and covered myself with moisturizer. Next came my favourite skinny jeans, a huge loose-knit jumper that I loved even though it had a hole in the shoulder, and big socks. Finally I sat on the floor in front of my mirror and blow-dried my hair, parting it into sections like they do at the hairdresser's. A slick of Frizz-Ease, and I was ready.

I got my phone and, sitting on my bed, composed

a text. Cool and breezy was the way forward. Anything heavy would just scare him off even more.

> Hi Joe. Thanx for fab
> wkend of rudeness ;)
> Have good week. Sx

I stood up, smoothed my duvet, and went downstairs to raid the fridge. I was starving.

At school the next day I was back to my old self, at least on the outside. Good old low-maintenance Sarah. I saw Ollie walking ahead of me and ran to catch him, linking my arm through his.

'Oh, all right, Sarah,' said Ollie, surprised. 'You OK?'

'Yeah.' I rested my head on his shoulder. 'I'm sorry about yesterday. I was a bitch.'

Ollie shrugged, bouncing my head up like a football. 'Don't worry about it. I was prob'ly an insensitive wanker. Joe call, did he?'

I shook my head. 'Nope, not yet.'

'Oh. Right.' Ollie paused while his boy brain tried to digest this latest non-development.

'Anyway,' he continued, 'you coming to Jack's big match tonight?'

We squeezed past a bunch of Year Sevens sitting in the stairwell sighing over a newspaper story about Justin Bieber. I almost envied them.

'Yeah, all right,' I said, in answer to Ollie's question. 'Is everyone going?'

He held open our tutor-room door. 'After you.' We sat down. A few others were dotted around, but Ollie and I were the first of our group.

'Ashley's got to work and Cass is seeing Adam,' he continued. 'But Donna and Rich are coming.' He drummed his knees under the table. 'Anyway. Glad you're feeling better, flower.'

'Yep, much better, thanks,' I said, trying to ignore the little hammer in my brain that was like a metronome, every beat an image of Joe: Joe at Victoria when he met me on Saturday morning, Joe's naked body, Joe's face as he came, Joe when he left me at the station. Especially Joe when he left me at the station.

'Uh, Sarah?' said Ollie.

'Yeah?'

'Jack's talking to you?'

I looked up to find everyone else had arrived. I really needed to get on top of the zoning-out thing. It was embarrassing. 'Sorry, Jack. What did you say?'

'Just that it's good you're coming tonight.'

I smiled brightly. 'Oh yeah. Wouldn't miss it.'

'Cool.' He peered at me, as if he was worried I'd blow at any second.

'What?' I laughed. 'I'm fine!' Judging by the sceptical looks around me, no one was convinced.

'Honestly! Look, I just zoned out for a minute. I'm not going mental or anything.'

Donna raised an eyebrow. 'And are we allowed to talk about the Joe thing?'

I shrugged. 'If you want.'

Cass still looked worried, bless her. 'Are you sure you're OK, hon? I mean, this is us.' She gestured around the table. 'You don't have to pretend.'

'What? I'm not pretending!' This was beginning to piss me off. 'Look, it's true I was gutted after I left Joe on Sunday, but it was my own fault. I just read too much into it. End of. It was still an amazing weekend . . .' I lowered my voice. 'We still had amazing sex.' I looked pointedly at Ashley and Donna.

Ash spread her hands. 'Fair play, Sar. I can respect that.'

'Me too.' Donna came round the table and gave me a hug. 'I'm glad you're OK.'

'Yeah, we didn't like sad Sarah,' said Cass, smiling at me.

'So does this mean we can get pissed tonight to celebrate?' asked Rich, rubbing his hands together.

'It's always when I have to work,' moaned Ashley. 'Can't we do it this weekend instead?'

'Aw, babes, we'll do it then too,' said Rich. 'Why don't you tell your mum that you can't work tonight?'

'Right. Like that's an option,' said Ashley bitterly. Her mum owns a designer wedding dress boutique in The Lanes and they do fittings in the evenings. Ash has to wipe off her eyeliner, put on a suit and make nice with brides-to-be and their rich mummies. It's ironic, cos the shop doesn't make Ash's mum rich. Pretty much the opposite, in fact. Bad time for the economy, and all that.

'Me and Adam are having a night in,' said Cass, looking disappointed. 'But if I finish my Spanish translation in time I'll definitely come out at the weekend.'

Rich put his arms round me and Donna. 'Looks like it's just me and ma bitches then.'

'And Jack and Ollie,' I reminded him.

'Yes, they are my bitches too,' he agreed, and then ducked as various missiles came at him from Ollie and Jack's direction.

I had such lovely friends. Why couldn't they be enough for me? I sighed and turned to the front as Paul finally arrived to count us in and read out the day's notices. *Tonight will be good*, I told myself. *Just focus on that.*

And, actually, it was good. To start with anyway.

From the moment the teams ran on to the pitch, we knew it was Jack's night. He was on fire. Even I

82

could tell he was all over the other team, ducking and diving and basically being a total hero. Me, Donna, Ollie and Rich leapt about on the sidelines, cheering like loons.

'Drink, anyone?' Rich held out a hip flask.

'Don't mind if I do,' said Donna, unscrewing the lid and reeling back before she'd even taken a mouthful. 'Ugh, what the hell is that?'

Rich shrugged. 'Calvados. It was either that or wine. And only winos put wine in a hip flask.'

'You know you don't always have to siphon off your parents' alcohol. You could just buy stuff like a normal person,' said Donna, taking a swig and wincing, then contemplating the flask appreciatively. 'Huh. Nice burn.'

'I know, right?' Rich nodded enthusiastically, as if he'd fermented the stuff himself.

Donna passed the flask to Ollie, who took a couple of sips then passed it to me. I didn't even think. I just drank. 'Oh God, that's disgusting.' It tasted like medicine-flavoured fire, and not in a good way. I stuck my tongue out and flapped at it to take away the burn.

'Whoa, Sarah, drinking on a school night?' Donna grinned and gave me an atta-girl arm punch. 'Nice one, babes. Do you good.'

I hoped so. I was about to pass the flask back to

Rich when something stopped me. Sod it. I took another swig. And another.

By the end of half-time, I was hammered. But it was fine. Great, even. I was having the best time. Everything was Jack, and the boys, and Donna, and resolutely, definitely, positively not Joe.

The whistle blew for the start of the second half and we turned our attention back to the match. I jogged about on the spot as Jack weaved through the other players towards the goal. 'C'MON, JACK!' I bellowed. I turned and started conducting an imaginary choir. 'Two, four, six, eight, who do we appreciate?' I chanted, then paused and grinned expectantly at the others.

Rich laughed and shook his head. *No cheerleading*, he mouthed. *Not cool.*

'What?' I was flabbergasted. 'Cheerleading rocks!' I started high-kicking and waving imaginary pom-poms. 'C'mon, people, get with the cheerleading programme!' I tugged at Donna's coat. 'Donna. Donna. DONNA. Cheerlead with me. DONNA!'

She gently prised my fingers from her sleeve. 'All right, Sar, maybe calm down, yeah? It's getting a bit annoying, babes.'

I shrugged and turned back to the match. They were always on at me to lighten up, and here I was, light as a freakin' feather. I danced about on the

84

sidelines, shouting encouragement to Jack, then turned to Rich but he shook his head and held the flask out of reach. 'Sweet-pea, you're hammered.'

I gave him a *duh* face. 'No! Really?' I jumped up to grab the flask, but Rich pushed me away with a gentle shove to the forehead.

'Look, much as I'm loving new crazy drunkard Sarah, I think you've had enough,' he said. 'This is a bad idea, believe me.' I slumped and nodded, then lunged as soon as Rich started to put the flask back in his pocket.

'HA! Gotcha,' I crowed, holding the flask up for a second before throwing my head back and downing the lot. 'Aw. All gone,' I said, holding the flask upside down.

'Thank God for that,' said Donna. 'Sit down, will you, before you fall over.'

But I was one step ahead of her. My legs suddenly buckled and I fell heavily to the floor.

'Ow, that hurts,' I said, tears of pain stinging my eyes. And you know how one tear can spark a flood? A second later, it was as if all the grief in the world was on my shoulders.

'Oh, babes,' sighed Donna, squatting down and putting her arms round me. I rested my head on her shoulder and howled.

7

'All done?'

I nodded and wiped my mouth with the back of my hand. We were in the bathroom at Donna's house, and I had spent the last forty-five minutes puking up a potent cocktail of Calvados and the chicken burger and chips I'd had earlier. I turned and sat on the bath mat, my back against the bath. Donna joined me, wisely taking the side furthest from the toilet.

'I'm really sorry,' I said, putting my head in my hands.

'I know, babes, you've told me, like, a million times.'

I peered at her through my fingers. She was staring straight ahead, her expression neutral. She didn't look angry, but you could never tell with Donna and you didn't want to get on the wrong side of her. Ours is not a friendship based on similar personalities. She's a laid-back, fly-by-the-seat-of-her-pants, what-you-see-is-what-you-get kind of girl. I'm pretty much the opposite. But despite or, I dunno, maybe because of this, we get on. She's fun, and nice, and I like her honesty. And tonight she'd somehow got me to her house, persuaded her dad to let me stay, and held my hair back while I'd surrendered my stomach contents to the porcelain god.

I was having a severe attack of the guilts. 'I don't deserve you,' I said, shaking my head.

'Piss off,' said Donna, good-naturedly. She examined her nails. 'And stop worrying about it. Happens to the best of us.'

I sighed. 'Not to me it doesn't.'

She laughed. 'Yeah, well, about time it did.'

We sat in silence for a minute. I looked around for my phone. 'What time is it?'

'Probably close to midnight. And your bag's downstairs.'

I tried to stand up, but the room started spinning crazily so I sat down again. 'Are you sure it's OK to stay tonight?' I rested my cheek against the cool side of the bath. I was feeling sick again.

'Yeah, Dad's fine with it,' Donna replied, eyeing me warily. 'You OK?'

I nodded, although I wasn't convinced.

'I need to call my parents.'

'Don't worry, I already texted your mum from your phone. You told her Jack's team won so we'd come here to celebrate and as it was late you were going to stay the night.'

'Oh, thanks, Don,' I said, relieved I had one less thing to worry about. 'Did she reply?'

Donna smiled at me. 'Dunno. You started vom-ming.' I smiled what I believe books call ruefully and had another go at standing up. Donna took my hand. 'Careful. Take it slowly.' She kept hold of me as I gin-gerly followed her into the bedroom she used to share with her sister until last year, when Jess left home. Donna pushed all the books, DVD cases, clothes and magazines that were piled on Jess's bed on to the floor. 'Hop in.' I gratefully crawled on to the delicious, cool sheet, and Donna covered me with the duvet. I'd worry in the morning about what clothes to wear to school.

I smiled dopily, my eyes already closing. 'Fanks, Don.' I felt the mattress dip as Donna sat next to me on the bed. She stroked my hair away from my eyes.

'No probs, babes. Any time.'

But I was already asleep.

I woke the next day to broad daylight. Donna's cur-tains were open and her duvet hastily flung over her sheets, which is what passes for making the bed in Donna-land. I listened. The house was empty. I sat up and clutched my head. Ow. My first proper hang-over. My mouth felt like sandpaper that someone had used to wipe their bum. I gingerly lay back down, and something crackled under my head. I felt behind me, grunting with the effort, and grabbed a piece of paper between my fingers.

S. Left you to sleep it off. Dad's at work. Help
yourself to shower, clothes, food!!
   Later, dude. D xxx

I groaned. Not only did I never get drunk, especially
on a school night, but I also never bunked off, and
this was my second sicky in a week. *Joe's doing this to
you*, said a little voice in my head. *You're better off without
him.* I ignored it. I was better off WITH him. That
was the whole point. Duh.

I stumbled out of bed and into the bathroom,
which still stank of sick. I groaned again. I doubted
I'd ever be able to look Donna's dad in the eye again,
although he was the most liberal of all our parents –
he'd bought Donna an eighth of weed for her
birthday – so maybe he wouldn't care. I really hoped
not. Parents liked me. I had a kind of head-screwed-
on vibe that they went for.

I carefully locked the bathroom door and fiddled
with the shower dial. A jet of freezing cold water hit
my arm. Shit shit shit. Whatever I did, the water
wouldn't heat up. In the end I took the shower head
out of its holder and blasted the neediest parts of my
anatomy as quickly as I could. At least it cleared my
head a bit.

Back in Donna's room I kept my towel wrapped
round myself with one hand and opened her knicker

drawer with the other. I grabbed a pair of plain black socks and the first boring-looking pair of high-legs I found (Donna had a strict pants hierarchy: plain high-legs at the bottom, thongs in the middle, shorts with matching bra at the top) and put on my own bra. Next I opened her wardrobe. She's much taller and curvier than me (eat your heart out, Beyoncé – seriously), but I found a smallish sweatshirt and a pair of jeans that I turned up at the bottom. They would look completely wrong with the ballet pumps I was wearing yesterday, but I told myself firmly that it was the price I paid for being such a dirty stop-out. Thus attired, I gathered up my own smelly clothes and went downstairs.

My bag was leaning against the bottom step. I found my phone and felt a little stab of hope as I brought it to life. Three texts. My heart thumping, I opened my Messages box. One was from Mum, saying she'd see me tonight, one was from Donna, and one was from Ollie wanting to know how I was. I hadn't really expected anything different, but still. I sighed and wandered into the kitchen. I wanted to eat something, but nothing appealed. There was a can of Diet Coke in the fridge, but it felt wrong taking the only one. I took a couple of Hobnobs from the biscuit jar, picked up my bag and opened the front door. I didn't want to go to school and face everyone. I didn't really want to do anything except sleep. I felt like shit, and not just from the booze. I slapped my own face. *For God's sake, woman, pull yourself together.* With a shake of my shoulders, which did nothing at all to make me feel better, I shut the door behind me and started trudging in the direction of school.

I was concentrating so hard on not giving in to the nausea that was once again washing over me that I didn't hear my phone ringing until it was almost too late. I grabbed it on the final ring and, without looking to see who it was, pressed the button to answer.

''lo?'

'All right?'

I almost dropped the phone. A wave of happiness, confusion and a fleetingly urgent need to be sick struck me dumb.

'Er, Sarah, you there?'

'Yeah. Sorry. Just dropped my phone.' I waited for him to speak. I'd practised this moment enough times to know I had to let Joe do the talking.

'So. How's it going?' He sounded completely normal. As if Sunday afternoon at the station had never happened.

'Not bad, thanks. Bit of a hangover.' I kept my voice even.

'Bummer. Anyway. Me and the boys are coming to Brighton this weekend. Will's having a house party at his parents' house.'

'Oh, right.' (*Keep it slow, Sarah*, I told myself. *Don't get excited.*)

'So. D'you want to come?' He lowered his voice. 'I've been thinking about you.'

My stomach flipped, this time not from the hangover. Every fibre of my being was screaming at me to say I'd go, but instead I screwed up my eyes and said, 'Ah, damn, I'm supposed to be going out with my friends this weekend.'

'Bring them too. More the merrier,' said Joe breezily.

'Uh. Yeah, OK.' It was the best I could do in my current state.

'Cool. I'll text you the details. See you then, Sarah Doesn't-like-beer.' And my phone beeped to tell me he'd ended the call. I stared at it for a second. Looked like I was seeing Joe this weekend then.

I was going to see Joe! I did a little jump, and instantly regretted it when the Hobnobs threatened to reappear. Suddenly my headache was just the price I was paying for a top night out, and the low, grey clouds were lined with silver. I walked the rest of the way to school with as much spring in my step as a Calvados hangover would allow.

8

Donna came in slightly late to tutor group and pretty much strutted to her seat. I'd been waiting for her to arrive before asking everyone to come to the party on Saturday, but from the smug look on her face I guessed she was going to pip me to the post on the news front.

'You're looking pleased with yourself,' said Rich. 'Got something you want to tell us?'

Ashley rolled her eyes. 'Don't encourage her, Richard.'

'I have, actually,' said Donna, giving Ashley the old scratch-cheek-with-middle-finger manoeuvre. She rummaged in her bag, pulled out an envelope and wafted it like a flag. 'Free tickets to a Bombay Bicycle Club gig, anyone?'

Jack frowned. 'Never heard of them.'

'That's not the point, is it?' she replied, shaking her head pityingly. 'It's a free night out.' She eyed us all. 'Who's in?'

'When is it?' asked Cass.

Donna sighed as if we were spoiling everything

with our pointless questions. 'Saturday? When we were all going to get together anyway? Come on, people – it's free!'

This Saturday? 'Oh no, that's Joe's party!' I bit my lip. 'I was just about to tell you about it. He phoned this morning and invited us all to his friend Will's party. It's here in Brighton . . .' There was an awkward silence.

'Free tickets, hon,' said Cass pleadingly. 'That doesn't happen every day. Can't you see Joe next weekend?'

'Not really,' I said, trying not to sound sulky. 'It's not that easy for us, is it?'

'We'll come out next time, babes. Promise,' said Rich, and Ollie and Jack chipped in with much the same.

'My dad'll be gutted if we don't use the tickets,' added Donna, finally. 'He was well excited that his client had given them to him.'

(I'd never been sure what Donna's dad did for a living, and now it was too late into our friendship to ask. Something to do with cars, maybe? I really had no idea.)

'Oh look, I'll go with you, Sar,' said Ashley, making everyone turn wide eyes on her as if she'd just admitted to being secretly male or something.

I blinked with disbelief. 'Really? Are you sure?'

There was a slight pause – long enough for my heart to start sinking. I so didn't want to turn up at a party full of strangers on my own. But then she said: 'Yeah. I like Bombay Bicycle Club, but I suppose I feel bad about not being there for you last night . . .' She smirked. 'Can't miss out on another opportunity of seeing Drunken Sarah in action, can I?'

'Ugh. Never again,' I said, wincing. 'But thank you, you're brilliant.'

She shrugged. 'I know . . . And I suppose there's also a *slight* possibility that I want to meet this Joe dude.'

I smiled gratefully. 'Cheers, Ash.'

So on Saturday evening, while everyone else went to the gig, Ashley came round and sat on my bed while I agonized over what to wear.

'Oh God, I have nothing,' I wailed, sitting cross-legged in bra and knickers in a sea of jeans, tops and skirts.

'Yeah, you do. What about that?' Ashley pointed towards a Seventies-style denim skirt I'd bought a few months before and never worn. I shook my head.

'Makes me look like a librarian.'

She swung her fishnets-and-biker-boot-clad legs. 'Not if you wear it with, like, wedges and an ironic blouse.'

'An ironic blouse?' I gaped in disbelief. 'And I don't own any bloody wedges.'

'OK then, let's start with the shoes.' Ash sat up. 'What do you have?'

I looked around me. 'Converse, flip-flops, knee boots, ballet pumps and those.' I pointed at a vile pair of lilac satin stilettos I'd had to wear last year as a bridesmaid at my cousin's wedding.

Ash frowned. 'Yeah, no. It's not a great list, is it?'

How helpful. This was ridiculous. I was going to a student's house party, not the bloody Oscars. I pulled on my favourite skinny jeans and a floaty tunic top from Zara, then stepped into my newest ballet pumps. 'Done.' I stood with my hand on my hip and glared at Ash.

'All right, scary pants,' she laughed. 'Good choice. You look lovely. Can we go now?'

We walked to the pub where Joe had said they were all meeting. Ashley strode ahead while I lagged behind, feeling nervous. 'C'mon, keep up,' Ash called behind her. 'Or they'll have gone by the time we get there.' I trotted beside her.

'Aren't you scared of all those new people?' I asked.

Ash glanced at me. 'No.'

'How'd you do it?' I really wanted to know.

She shrugged. 'Pretend. They don't know you're cacking yourself, so pretend you're not . . . It's how my mum does it when she has to sell five-grand wedding dresses to rich people. She says at the beginning she was so in awe of their, like, Porsches and manicures and Chanel handbags that she could hardly talk to them. But now they assume she's as rich as they are.'

I mused on that one. It had never occurred to me that Ash was anything other than naturally sociable.

'Course, it helps if you're a bit pissed,' added Ashley.

Oh. 'I'm not going down that road again.' My mouth twisted with memory nausea. Ash nudged me affectionately.

'Aw, Sarah, you're such an amateur . . . It's cute, really.'

I harrumphed and said nothing. Cute was not something I aspired to.

'Bugger.' Ash stopped in her tracks as we approached the pub. 'They're checking ID.'

My heart sank. 'Do you have any?'

'Always. Do you?' But she already knew the answer. 'Look, just work out your date of birth before you get there and tell them you left your wallet at home. It'll be fine.'

I wasn't convinced. I have a fresh-faced thing

going on, and I don't wear much make-up. Ash probably didn't need ID, with her smudgy eyes and crazy dyed hair. But I was pretty sure I would. We stood a bit straighter and marched up to the door.

'All right, ladies,' said the black-clad bouncer. 'Can I see your ID please?'

Ashley showed her skilfully faked Brighton Uni card and was waved through. I tossed my hair and imagined I was Joe's bitchy friend Mimi. 'Oh God, I left mine at home,' I rah'ed. Apparently eighteen-year-old me is posh. Who knew? 'Look, I'm five oh-one ninety-three,' I said. 'I'm nearly nineteen, for goodness' sake!' I laughed in what I hoped was a relaxed and mature manner.

The bouncer shook his head. 'Sorry, no ID: no entry.' And that was that. He had already moved on to the person behind me. Ash squeezed past the successfully ID'd people who were now breezily entering the pub and came back out to join me in pariah land.

'What do we do now?' I said, pacing up and down the pavement.

'No need to panic,' said Ash smoothly. 'Just text Joe to say we're running late and ask for his friend's address.'

I nodded manically. 'Oh, good idea, I'll do that.' Ash shook her head in despair at my total lack of cool and sat on the kerb, patting the space beside her. I sat down and sent the text. Coincidentally I heard someone in the group of people who'd just left the pub get a text at the same time. Shit! I grabbed Ash's wrist. 'Look down!' I hissed. 'It's him.'

Ash craned her neck. 'Where?'

I almost cried. 'Please look down, Ash,' I whispered. 'He'll know we got ID'd if he sees us here.' I didn't care so much if Joe knew, but what if his bitchy friends were there? They'd think it was hilarious, and I couldn't bear that.

'All right, all right,' hissed Ashley back at me. She peered up through her fringe. 'Which one's Joe?'

'Suede jacket,' I replied through gritted teeth. 'Light brown hair.'

'Nice arse,' she said, appreciatively. 'Anyway, they've gone now. You can come out of hiding.'

I slowly looked up to see the tail end of his group turning a corner ahead of us. I closed my eyes and slowly exhaled. What the hell was happening to me?

'You all right, babes?' Ash looked concerned, and slightly amused.

I slapped my knees and stood up. 'Yes, thank you, fine now.' I held up my phone. 'I've got the address. Let's go.'

It was a short walk to Will's parents' place. It was in a leafy avenue of big, expensive houses, and not at all like my idea of a student house.

'This is it.'

We stopped outside a huge, white-painted three-storey Victorian place. It was like something out of Mary Poppins. Ash gazed in awe, finally murmuring, 'Spoonful of sugar or what?'

I looked at her and laughed. 'I was thinking the exact same thing.'

She hooked her arm through mine. 'C'mon then, let's go and violate Mr Banks.' I made retching noises and we ran, giggling, up the front steps.

It was heaving. There were people everywhere: sitting on the stairs, lounging against the walls, dancing around the living room, sitting around a dark wooden table in the dining room, leaning against the worktops in the kitchen. Everyone was drinking and loads of people were smoking. I wondered what Will's parents would think about the stench of old fags. No one stopped to ask who we were. I felt massively out of place.

'Cool party,' said Ash, nodding her head appreciatively to the music coming from the living room. It was some indie band I'd never heard of, but Ash obviously recognized it. She led me into the kitchen. 'Let's get a drink.'

An expensive-looking white and metal table was laden with wine and vodka. Under the table were two dustbins full of ice and bottles. I spotted a glimpse of white through all the brown and picked out a Smirnoff Ice. That'd do. Ash sloshed a generous measure of vodka into a plastic cup and topped it up with Coke. 'Cheers,' she said, holding up her drink while looking around the room. 'Whose place did you say this was again?'

'It's mine,' said a voice behind me. I watched Ashley's eyes widen at the sight of the voice's owner. I looked round.

'Hi, Will,' I said.

He smiled at me briefly. 'Hey, Sarah, how's it going?' But he was looking at Ash. How does she DO that?

'I'm Ashley,' she said, sticking her hand out. 'Seems you're Will.' She gazed up at him with huge eyes and a dirty grin, a mixture of pure sex and little-girl-lost. It was highly effective. Will nodded once, as if to say, *Ah yes, my reputation as a Greek god precedes me.*

'Where's Joe?' I asked quickly.

Will gestured through the wall to the dining room. 'In there.'

'Right. Well. I'll go and find him then.' I started to ask Ashley if she'd be OK, but it was a stupid question. She briefly caught my eye and mouthed, *Have fun.* I knew *she* would.

I squeezed through the crush, apologizing about a million times for treading on people's toes, and found my way into the dining room. Joe was sitting on the table, his feet on a chair, chatting to a bunch of people including, I was disgusted to note, bloody Mimi. I stood for a moment to watch them, but he spotted me almost immediately. His face broke into a massive smile and he jumped off the table and came over to me, wrapping me in a huge hug. My already shaky resolve weakened further. Oh, the smell of him.

'I'm so glad you came,' he shouted above the din. Then put his mouth to my ear and said, 'Fancy going upstairs and coming all over again?'

Even while my whole body cried out for me to say yes, I disengaged from his arms and stood back a bit. I wasn't quite besotted or stupid enough to jump into bed again after what happened at the station. And, anyway, where would we go? He must have sensed my hesitation, because he ran his hands up and down my arms and said, 'Look, Sarah, I'm sorry about what happened before . . . I was a bit scared, to be honest with you.' I stared at him sceptically and he took my arm, leading me into a corner of the room. 'Look, I haven't felt this way about anyone in a long time.' He ran the back of his hand down my cheek. 'You're beautiful, and funny, and clever . . . but you're young.'

I started to point out that I was only three years younger than him, but he stopped me. 'I know, I know. And you're mature for your age. But it does make a difference.' He glanced over at Mimi and I followed his gaze. She was glaring at me with such venom I would have laughed if I hadn't felt so scared. 'Some people don't think I should be seeing you,' Joe continued. 'But I can't help it.' He gently kissed my mouth. 'Please come upstairs with me. I can't talk to you here.'

'All right,' I said. 'But just to talk.'

Joe nodded and smiled, but his face was sincere. 'Whatever you want.' He took my hand and we made our way up the stairs. He stopped outside a closed door, gave it a quick knock then opened it and peered in. 'It's empty.' He beckoned me in and closed the door behind me.

'What if someone comes in?' I asked, taking in the two single beds, the *Toy Story* curtains and the toy wigwam in the corner.

'Somehow I don't think anyone's going to be sleeping here tonight,' Joe replied, jumping on to one of the beds and stretching out his legs.

I perched on the edge of the other bed. 'Where are Will's parents?'

'They've gone to the Bahamas for a month. This is his twin brothers' room.'

I looked around. 'Er, no offence, but isn't this room a bit immature for a twenty-year-old man?'

Joe looked confused for a second, then laughed. 'No, doofus. His little brothers who are twins?'

'Oh!' I reddened slightly and giggled. 'Blimey, Will's parents must be rich.' I fingered the embroidery on the nautical-striped bedspread.

Joe nodded. 'Yup.' Then he added cryptically, 'Old money.'

'Oh, right,' I said, not knowing what he meant. Joe stuck his leg out and gently tapped my leg with his toe.

'So, Sarah Doesn't-like-beer . . .' I didn't say anything, just sat and looked at him. 'Come and sit with me,' Joe wheedled. 'I promise I won't jump your bones. Much as I want to.' He eyed me so saucily that I couldn't help laughing. He scooted up and put his arm out, then snuggled me into him as I sat beside him. 'See? Much better.' The seconds ticked away. It was so nice to be with him again. I inhaled slowly, breathing in his scent.

'Uh, sorry, are you . . . *smelling* me?' He sounded shocked. I giggled. 'Well, how do I smell?' he asked.

I didn't miss a beat. 'Like shit.' Joe threw his head back and laughed.

'Oh, very funny, missy,' he said, tickling me. I writhed around, guffawing helplessly. I knew what he was trying to do, but I was past trying to stop it. And, yes, within seconds he had me pinned to the bed.

'Can I kiss you now?' he asked, his face sweetly hopeful. I pretended to think about it for a moment, then nodded.

'Thank God for that.'

I didn't stop him then, or when he undid my jeans, or when he shucked off his own jeans. I didn't even worry about the fact we were in an unlocked room. I wanted him. And, almost before I knew it was going to happen, we were having sex on the carpet.

I woke up to an empty room. Again. I sighed, then pulled the duvet up to my chin and looked around wildly. This was a bloody strange situation. I was lying on the carpet of a child's bedroom in a house whose owners didn't know me from Adam, with only a sailing boat bedspread covering my nakedness. I jumped up, hurriedly pulled my clothes on and made the bed as neatly as I could. I could still hear the party going on downstairs, which was a relief. I couldn't bear the thought of sneaking out of an empty house in the middle of the night. I checked my phone: it was just past one. I listened at the door to make sure no one was standing outside, then quickly slipped on to the landing.

Where the hell was Joe? I hurried past closed doors, hoping to find one that looked like it belonged to a bathroom, but they all looked the same. Finally I found an open door with a toilet behind it. I gratefully used it, taking the opportunity to use the mirror and check I didn't look too much like a person who had just had sex. I smoothed my hair, then wet a bit of toilet roll under the tap and rubbed it under my eyes. The mascara smudges wouldn't budge. Giving up, I left the room and hurried downstairs. I wanted to find Joe and Ashley, in that order. But, of course, the first person I bumped into – literally – was Mimi.

'Watch it,' she snapped as I careered into her at the bottom of the stairs. Then, 'Oh, it's you.' She leant one hand against the wall so my exit was blocked. 'Nice fuck, was it?' she asked, smiling thinly. 'But oh! Where's Joe?' She looked behind me exaggeratedly.

'He's just gone to the loo,' I said, with as much dignity as I could muster.

Mimi laughed nastily. 'Yeah, right.' Then she leant into me so I had to back up a step. 'Listen, little girl,' she hissed. 'Joe is using you.' She emphasized every word. 'He's using you for your tight virginal little fanny and your breathless little-girl adoration.' I could only gawp. I couldn't believe that a fellow human being could be so utterly horrible.

'How do you know?' I asked hoarsely.

'What, that you were a virgin? He told me.' Her mouth curled into a smile as she saw my face fall and

she brought her hand up to her mouth in mock surprise, showing her perfectly manicured nails. 'Oops,
sorry, was it a secret? Cos you should know that it's
blatantly obvious to, like, everyone that you're Little
Miss Frigid. Sucked him off yet, by the way?' I didn't
answer, and she laughed in what she probably thought
was a light and tinkly manner, but actually sounded
like a witch cackling.

I was about to literally die of humiliation when
someone spoke behind me.

'And what's it to you?'

I spun round. It was Ashley. I almost cried with
relief. Mimi's expression didn't waver. She did that
dead-smile thing at me again and said, 'Getting your
friends to stand up for you. How sweet.' But, with
another glance at Ashley and a quick up-and-down
of disgust at me, she turned and stalked off. I sunk
down on to the step.

'Who the hell was that bitch?' asked Ash, sitting
beside me.

'Mimi. One of Joe's friends.' I dropped my head
on to my knees. 'She says he's using me.' I didn't mention the rest.

Ashley snorted briefly with laughter. 'Well, don't
bloody listen to her. She's obviously jealous . . . Where
is Joe, anyway?'

I shrugged helplessly. 'I don't know. I fell asleep

and when I woke up he'd gone.' Ashley didn't say anything, which spoke volumes. 'Where's Will?' I asked.

She leant back on her elbows. 'Dunno . . . I left while he was sleeping.' She looked at me and I burst out laughing. And then we were both cackling away on the stairs, the jilted and the jiltee, until suddenly I wasn't laughing any more.

9

I slept late the next day and woke to a text from Joe.

> Sorry missed u last nite.
> Will call soon. Xxx

I couldn't really see how leaving while I was asleep was 'missing' me, as if he'd gone to the bathroom and when he'd come back I'd gone . . . And then the thought struck me that, of course, that's exactly what could have happened. Mimi might have scoffed when I told her Joe had gone to the loo, but what if he had? That house probably had at least three bathrooms. I texted back:

> Me too. See u soon. Next
> weekend??? Xx

After spending what seemed like hours lying awake the night before wondering what to do about Mimi, I decided that it would be massively uptight of me to have a go at him for telling her about me. Firstly cos he wouldn't have told her about me if there was anything between them, and secondly because I didn't want him to know that she even slightly bothered me. Ashley was right: she was totally jealous of me. The thought made me feel kind of powerful. (*Pride comes before a fall*, piped up Annoying-voice-in-my-head.)

I went downstairs in my PJs to make some toast. Mum had left a note on the fridge:

Dan at Oscar's, dad at Tesco, me at gym!

So I had the house to myself. Bliss. I ate my toast while catching up on some social networking – I sent Joe a Facebook friend request – then ran a bath and soaked for an hour. I spent the afternoon making notes for an Art History essay and doing my French translation. With all homework done by the time the rest of my family were home, I ate my pasta bake with smug contentment, spent the evening watching crap TV and was in bed by ten. I didn't even care that Joe hadn't replied to my text. He'd already established his slow-reply credentials. I could wait him out.

I sat up in bed. Still, a quick call before sleep wouldn't hurt. I found him in my Contacts list and clicked Call. It went to answerphone and I left a breezy message saying how it'd had been fun yesterday and we should do it again soon.

Setting my alarm for morning, I fell asleep quickly. It had been a strangely satisfying day.

Joe didn't respond the next day. I couldn't stop thinking about what Mimi had said. Even if she was jealous, that didn't necessarily make her wrong. And part of me was still in shock that someone could hate me so much. I wasn't used to being disliked. It gave me a permanent sick feeling in my stomach, like suddenly realizing I'd missed a vital exam.

I asked Ashley to meet me on the playing field at lunchtime. I wanted to talk about Joe with someone who'd actually met him, not that I told her that. I got there first (of course), spread my coat on the grass and settled down to eat my sandwich. The weather had finally caught up with the season and it was properly chilly. After a minute I saw Ashley trudging towards me.

I shifted so she could share my coat. 'All right?' She nodded and sat down. She was using a ring binder spewing assorted notes and handouts as a tray, on top of which was a plate of chips from the canteen. 'How'd you smuggle that out?' I asked, taking a chip.

She smiled. 'Dunno. Just did.' It didn't surprise me. 'So. You all right?'

'Yeah, fine.' Even to my own ears it sounded false. The high-pitched squeak was a particularly nice touch. I cleared my throat. 'What did you think of Will, then?'

Ashley shook her head. 'He's hot as, but sadly he's also quite boring and not great in bed.' She put a chip in her mouth and spoke round it. 'Bit selfish, if you know what I mean. Had to finish myself off in the bathroom.'

'Ashley!' I was shocked.

'What?' Ash laughed at the look on my face. 'C'mon, babes, we all do it.' I reddened and looked away. I wasn't getting into that conversation.

'Anyway, have you heard from Joe?'

I nodded. 'He texted yesterday morning.' Then, casually 'What did you think of him, by the way?'

Ashley took a chip. 'Hard to say. I only saw him from a distance.'

I nodded eagerly. 'And?'

She shrugged. 'Yeah, he's good-looking.'

'He really is, isn't he?' I smiled at the thought of my gorgeous man, but then that condescending sneer popped into my head again. 'I can't stop thinking about what Mimi said, though.'

'What, that psycho? I think we can safely ignore everything she says.' Ashley smirked at the memory. 'God, she was well jealous of you.'

But I didn't think it was funny. It made me feel sick. 'But what if she was right? And she's so pretty and, like, groomed.'

Ash rolled her eyes. 'Jesus, give yourself a break . . . You've got a gorgeous smile, lovely big brown cow eyes – that's a compliment, by the way – and I'd kill for hair as thick as yours. AND he obviously fancies you . . . Even if he did leave you in the lurch.'

'No, that's not what happened. He went to the bathroom and I left before he got back,' I said quickly.

Ash raised an eyebrow. 'He tell you that, did he?'

'No,' I admitted. 'But he didn't need to.'

'Right,' she said enigmatically, stuffing more chips into her mouth. She wiped her greasy hands on her skirt. 'Still, I suppose he did text you yesterday. That's pretty good. For him.'

I ignored the pregnant pause and tried to smile. 'Exactly.' She was probably right – about him fancying me, I mean. Let's face it, she knew way more about this kind of thing than I did. Hell, everyone in the world knew more than I did.

I checked my phone for the time. 'We'd better get back.'

Ash nodded and clambered to her feet. 'Shit, remind me not to sit on the floor in a non-stretch miniskirt again.' She looked around. 'Not that I really care who sees my gusset.'

And there you had the difference between us in a nutshell.

*

But the next morning my mood was back to sub-zero. I'd left two more messages for Joe and had just got a text from him.

> Am working in bar so
> can't do weekends 4 a bit.
> Will call u xx

It made sense for him to get a job, and he couldn't exactly work during the week. But I felt snubbed. And I couldn't bear the thought that Mimi could see Joe every day at uni.

Mentally cursing my parents for not having the foresight to conceive me three years earlier, I plodded to school, stopping at the loos before I had to drag myself to the maths room for tutor group. Sitting in a cubicle staring mindlessly at a new bit of graffiti ('EC has a bucket fanny' – nice), I was suddenly aware of familiar voices outside by the sinks.

'I can't believe he shagged and ran.' It was Donna. I froze, my heart thumping.

Then Ashley's voice. 'I know. She reckons he'd just gone to the bathroom and she left before he got back, but . . .' I could imagine her expression.

'He's so just in it for the sex.' Donna again.

'I know. Poor Sarah – she just can't see it. She's obsessed.' Cass was there too! I could sort of understand Ashley and Donna discussing me behind my back, but Cass? She was my best friend. She shouldn't be talking about me like this with them. And how dare she feel sorry for me! Talk about pot and kettle. I felt sick. I couldn't believe my friends thought I was deluded about Joe. Donna and Cass hadn't even met him and Ashley had only seen him, not properly talked to him.

Well, they could think what they wanted, I decided defiantly. They didn't know Joe like I did. But still, their words stung. I waited for a minute after they left before slipping out. It was still early for tutor, but I went anyway. I wasn't ready to face the girls.

In the tutor room I sank into a chair, barely acknowledging Ollie who had yet again arrived early. He appeared to have turned over a new leaf, time-keeping wise.

'You all right, McSarey?' he asked.

I sighed heavily. 'What is it with men, Ols?'

Ollie looked contrite. He placed his hand on his heart. 'On behalf of all penis-owners, I apologize,' and he seemed so genuinely sorry that I laughed. He twirled a Biro between his fingers. 'Joe issues?'

I chewed the inside of my cheek and nodded.

'Well, he's a dick if you ask me,' said Ollie, evenly. 'He's lucky to have you.'

I snapped my head up, but he was concentrating

on spinning his pen. I laughed nervously. 'Ol, you're the king of love 'em and leave 'em.'

He smiled. 'Yeah well, I just haven't met the right girl, have I?' He looked at me, his expression open. I relaxed. Last thing I needed was for bloody Ollie to get a crush on me. I coloured slightly at letting such a ridiculous thought even enter my head. We'd known each other since we were five. He'd shown me his teeny-weenie in the playground and I'd seen him cry when he'd fallen over. He was sweet and kind and funny, but he was Ollie. Burp king and serial shagger. And, anyway, why on earth would he fancy me? I leant across the table and gave him a hug.

'Thanks, Ol.'

He shrugged and smiled. 'Anytime, flower.'

The morning dragged like wading through water. I had French, which was fine but I wasn't in the mood, and then a free period, which I spent in the library doing research for my art-history essay. Boring boring boring. As the clock hands dragged themselves towards lunchtime, my mind kept drifting away from the use of painterly techniques in the work of Jackson Pollock and on to a way more pressing dilemma. What to do? Should I avoid the girls (my favoured option), or swan into the canteen casually as if nothing was wrong (not ideal, but the non-confrontational side of me was all for it)? As upset as I was, avoiding them would only be putting off the inevitable. So – *sigh* – facing up to them it was.

Although obvs I wouldn't do any *actual* facing up. That would most definitely be classed as confrontation. All I needed to do was show my face. Be normal. Not 'obsessed'. It hurt that they thought that about me, but at the same time I kind of knew how they felt. I was beginning to annoy myself. I scuffed my toe against the floor irritably as I waited for the ancient PC to log me off. Why couldn't Joe just *arrange* to see me? Did it always have to be last minute? I reminded myself that not everyone was as obsessed with planning ahead as I was. But still. A *bit* of planning couldn't hurt.

The canteen was nearly empty when I got there, but Cass and Jack were sitting at our usual table. They both had Spanish before lunch on a Tuesday – they must have been let out early. I bought a pasta salad and my usual Ribena and went to join them.

Cass started talking before I'd even sat down. 'Sarah, what are you doing over half term?'

I stared at her. 'What?'

'The boys are planning a trip to Devon. I was just thinking we could borrow Charlie's car and go too.' Cass's brother was, like, twenty-five, but he still lived at home. He was supposed to be doing a part-time IT course, but he never seemed to be doing anything except eating crisps and doing suspect things on the Internet. But, handily for us, he had a car. Even better, he never used it.

'Well, I might be seeing Joe,' I said, before I could stop myself. 'But we wouldn't be going for the whole week, right?' I added quickly. 'I could just see him the other days.' Even as I said it I knew that if Joe asked I'd blow my friends out to see him. It wasn't like that would always be the case. Just for now, while he was so busy with work and uni and I had to take any opportunity that arose. Cass should understand that better than anyone.

'Exactly,' said Cass, casually getting a notebook and pen from her bag as if the conversation in the loos had never happened. 'I'll be doing the same with Adam.'

I couldn't help feeling just a tiny bit smug. Cass might get to see Adam all the time, but at least Joe was faithful. Or why would that Mimi girl be so jealous?

'So, I'll put you down as a yes, yes?' Cass had her pen poised. I saw that she'd written 'Trip to Devon' at the top of the page and underlined it twice. The girl does love a list.

'Yes,' I said. 'Although obvs I'll have to check with my parents.'

'And, Jack, you're a yes?'

Jack laughed. 'Well, since it's our trip you're crashing . . .'

Cass scratched her forehead with her pen. 'Oh duh, of course. Sorry.' She wrote all the boys' names down and added hers and mine underneath. 'This is going to be such a giggle,' she said, tapping her pen on the table excitedly. 'We haven't done anything like this since Glastonbury.'

Jack nodded enthusiastically. 'Exactly what we said.' He started chuckling to himself. 'Rich and that stoned girl.' Cass burst out laughing and I smiled. God, that really had been funny. Rich had spent about two hours trying to give this random girl the slip. She was off her face and kept telling Rich he had a beautiful soul then trying to stick her tongue down his throat. I started laughing too. Cass and Jack's enthusiasm was infectious. I felt a flutter of excitement. Maybe a holiday with my friends was exactly what I needed. Get away from all the Joe stuff and just hang out together.

'What's so funny?' Rich pulled out a chair and sat down, closely followed by Ollie, Donna and Ashley.

'We were just remembering your Glastonbury girlfriend,' giggled Cass.

Rich rolled his eyes. 'Oh God, don't remind me. She was awful. And she stank of marzipan.'

I poked his arm. 'She wasn't to know you hate almonds.'

'Sweetheart, nobody in their right mind likes almonds. It's what cyanide smells of.'

We all laughed. We'd told this story a million times, always in the same way. It was a little flag in the map of our friendship.

The conversation moved on to Devon. When we'd go, how we'd get there. We all leant in to the table and offered suggestions while Cass made her lists. After a while I tuned out. Maybe me and Joe could go somewhere next summer. Maybe even back to Spain. I looked at my phone. No messages. I tapped out a quick text.

> Just thinking about u &
> spain dot dot dot . . .

I snickered to myself as I hit Send. He'd like this one. And, sure enough, a message pinged back a few minutes later.

> Dot dot dot indeed, dirty
> girl. I might phone u
> later. Much later . . .

I bit my lip. Was he talking about phone sex? I didn't even really know what phone sex involved, although I could make a pretty good guess. Making a mental note to Google it later, and a further mental note to erase my Internet history afterwards, I put my phone away. I wriggled in my chair. I was going to be thinking about sex with Joe for the rest of the day. Not ideal when I was about to go to English, although I bet Jane Eyre felt the same about Mr Rochester. And I'd take the horn over abject misery any day. (Yeah, high five, Jane. We're totally on the same page.)

I sat next to Rich in English, as usual. Mr Roberts liked to spend the first half of every lesson telling us exactly what was written in black and white on the handouts we all had in front of us. A massive waste of thirty minutes, which we usually spent earnestly looking like we were making notes while actually writing notes to each other. Rich was brilliant at nodding enthusiastically at just the right moment then apparently scribbling screeds of inspired stuff. Of course, the other thing with writing notes to each other is that you can say stuff you wouldn't necessarily say out loud. Which I guess is why straight off Rich came out with: *So what gives with u and Joe, hmmmm?*

I raised an eyebrow and scribbled: *No holding back with u is there?*

Rich sniggered and wrote: *You know it.*

Me: *What do u want to know?*

Rich: *Is he your BOYFRIEND????*

Me: *We're seeing each other.*
Rich: *Riiiiiight.*
Me: *What's that mean??*
Rich: *Sarah & Joe, sitting in a tree . . .*
Me: *Sigh. So mature.*
Rich: *Seriously. U really like him?*
Me: *I do.*
Rich: *And he really likes u?*

I paused. Now that was more difficult. I sighed and scrawled: *Who knows?*

Rich looked at me, but I pretended to be concentrating on what Mr Roberts was saying. He scribbled something else, but I didn't look down. I wasn't sure how much I wanted to tell him. I knew that whatever I told him would get back to the others, and, even if Rich didn't judge me, the others would. And I hated the thought of being talked about, even if it was good stuff.

I saw Rich write something and underline it three times. I swivelled my eyes so I could read it without him noticing. *HAHA MADE U LOOK!!*

I stifled a laugh and scrawled, *Do u mind, am transfixed by Mr R's beauty.* Rich squeaked and Mr Roberts frowned across at us, but we both instantly adopted the bored-but-listening stance, and he looked away.

I quickly wrote: *I'm taking it as it comes. He's busy at uni etc. But we have gr8 time together & i think it's worth working at. OK????*

Immediately Rich replied with: *Whatever you want, girlfriend. We just don't want u to get hurt.*

We? So the boys had been talking about me too. I sighed and turned my attention back to the front of the classroom. I didn't want any drama, I just wanted Joe to like me as much as I liked him. Was it such a big thing to ask?

At the end of the lesson there was the usual synchronized turning on of phones. Mr Roberts was a notorious phone confiscator – if he so much as caught sight of one, it was his for the rest of the day. You always knew if someone was about to go into a lesson with him, cos they'd be turning their phone to Silent and burying it in the bottom of their bag to muffle any vibration.

I didn't have any messages, but Rich had a voicemail. 'Gimme a sec?' I nodded and he put his phone to his ear. I knew straight away that something was badly wrong. The colour drained from his face and his mouth set into a thin line, turned down at the corners.

I put my hand on his arm. 'Are you OK?' Stupid question. He blinked and cleared his throat.

'Uh. No, actually.' He did a strange, confused smile, as if what he was about to say was so freaky that it was almost funny. 'My nan died.'

'Oh, Rich. Oh no. Not Nanny Blue?' They were

really close, him and his nan. She'd looked after him until he was old enough to walk home from school by himself, and he still visited her all the time. He nodded and his chin wobbled, so I lightly pushed him forward. 'C'mon, let's get out of here.' We walked out of school and across the field in silence. He'd talk when he'd got it together.

'She died in the night,' he said, after a minute. 'They think she had a stroke. My granddad woke up next to her, and she was dead.'

I rubbed his back, not knowing what to say.

'Like, I know she was really old, but she wasn't ill. She was healthy . . .' His voice trailed off.

'I'm so sorry, Rich.'

He turned to me. 'The funeral's probably going to be on Friday. Will you . . .?'

I interrupted him. 'Course I'll come. We'll all be there. No question.'

Rich stopped walking and half turned in the direction of school. 'Actually, I'm OK. I just want to get on with it. D'you know what I mean?'

'I think I do,' I said. 'Do you want to be on your own?'

He shot me a quick, sad smile. 'Nah, you're OK.' He hooked his arm through mine. 'Come and be with me when I tell the others.'

*

He was really brave. There was a shaky moment when Jack wrapped him in a hug, but he held it together. On the way to find the others he'd called his mum – Nanny Blue was her mum – and had a short but heartbreaking conversation. His mum was obviously devastated, which was really hard for Rich. Poor him. I felt so sorry for him. I still had all my grandparents and had never lost anyone I loved, and the very thought scared the shit out of me. The more so cos I knew it'd have to happen one day.

Nanny Blue's funeral was definitely going to be on Friday. It would mean we'd have to miss school, but I was pretty sure my parents would be OK with it. Frankly, it was tough if they weren't. Anyway, Friday was the last day before half term, so it's not like we'd miss much.

I walked home with Cass, and of course we talked about Rich, but the closer I got to our house the more my thoughts turned to Joe, and phone sex. By the time I got in I was itching to get on the computer. I ran upstairs to my room then screeched to a comedy halt when I saw the empty space on my desk and remembered that my computer had broken. Mum had taken it to work to get one of the IT bods to fix it. I groaned out loud at the thought of having to use the family one. I could already hear tapping coming from the spare room: Daniel. Excellent.

I plastered on a smile as I popped my head round the door. 'All right, Dan? You going to be long?'

'Ages,' he said, without looking round. 'I'm doing my homework.'

God, he was SO irritating. And that so wasn't homework he was doing. 'Really? Does Mum know you're doing World of Warcraft at school?'

'Piss off, this is a history site.' I could see his cheekbones rise as he smirked to himself.

I swallowed the urge to shove his face into the screen. 'No, it isn't, dickhead. I'm not stupid.'

He sucked his teeth. 'See, if you're going to be rude I'm just going to have to stay on here all night.'

Screeching with frustration, I slammed the door and went back to my room. I could have dragged him off the chair – I was still stronger than him – but then he'd have pulled my hair, I'd have had to wrench his arm behind his back, he'd have gone crying to Mum . . . It just wasn't worth it. But that still left the phone-sex dilemma.

As it got later and later, I started to panic. What if Joe called me and I said completely the wrong thing? The humiliation would just about finish me off. In the end I barricaded myself in my room and called Ashley. She acted like she was asked that kind of thing all the time. I was so grateful I pretty much forgave her toilet tattling there and then.

'You say sexy stuff to each other while you both wank,' she said matter-of-factly. 'Why? Has Joe suggested it?'

'I'm not sure.' I read out his text.

'Sounds like it,' said Ashley. 'I take it you're up for it?'

'Um. Not sure,' I said again. 'We've never done . . . that when we're together.'

'Well, just ignore the call if you don't want to do it . . . Anyway, it might not be a bad idea to be, like, slightly less available.'

I fell back on my bed and looked at the glow-in-the-dark stars on the ceiling. 'God, Ash, how come everything's so simple for you?'

She was quiet for a moment. 'Dunno, babes. Maybe I just pick my battles.'

I remembered what she'd said on the night of the party, about pretending. 'Anyway. Thanks for the info. You're like my own personal sex dictionary.'

She laughed. 'You knows it. Have fun. Don't do anything I wouldn't do.'

She was still sniggering when I hung up.

In the end my problem was solved for me, because Joe didn't call anyway. Or, at least, not intentionally. I had finally fallen asleep at close to midnight only to suffer about a million dreams about phone sex. So to be woken by my phone ringing was disorientating, like waking up and discovering you really are naked in the exam room. My heart beating loudly, I squinted at the neon display: Joe.

'Hello?'

Nothing. I heard sporadic muffled sounds of talking, then a laugh. A female laugh. Properly awake now, I ended the call then immediately called him back. He answered on the fifth ring.

'Sarah?'

I cleared my throat. 'Oh, hi. Just returning your call.'

'Um, I didn't call you?' I heard giggling in the background.

'Um, yes you did? Check your phone. You called me just now.' I heard fumbling sounds.

'Oh. Right. So I did. Sorry, babe, I must have sat on it or something.' Further offstage hilarity.

'Who's that with you?' I asked, keeping my tone even.

'Oh. No one in particular.' His voice became less distinct. 'Say hi to Sarah.' Someone laughed and said something I couldn't catch. I thought I heard Joe shush them. Her. Whoever. I rested my cheek against the headboard. Oh well, while I had him on the phone . . .

'So. I was waiting for your call earlier,' I said, lightly. 'I'd put on my best PJs and everything.'

Joe cleared his throat. 'Yeah, sorry about that. We'll do it soon, yeah?'

Why couldn't his friends piss off and leave him to talk to me in peace? I hated the stilted way he spoke when they were around.

'I'm free tomorrow night,' I purred. I caught sight of myself in the mirrored wardrobe door and pulled a face. When did I become the kind of girl who phones a boy at two o'clock in the morning and makes cat noises at them?

He phoned me first, I reminded myself, even if it was by accident.

'Yes, that sounds goo–' he stopped. 'Ah no, I'm working . . .' He lowered his voice. 'Listen, I'll call you soon. I promise.' I started to respond, but he said, louder now, 'Look, I'd better go.' I only just had time to say a quick 'bye' before he ended the call.

I stared at my phone for a few seconds, its blank face suddenly all annoying and metaphorical. Was he with Mimi? It had sounded like her voice. Even though he'd told her about me, I hated that they were friends. HATED it. She was a vicious, evil bitch, and he was my gorgeous, sexy Joe. I was terrified that she'd get her claws into him, bewitch him with her stupid flicky hair and annoying laugh. I could hear Donna telling me to chill out – he'd chosen me, hadn't he? But the fact remained. Mimi was there with him. I was not.

10

People always talk about the weather when it comes to funerals, like if it's raining it's apt, if it's sunny it's ironic. But the weather on Friday was totally schizo, raining one minute, sunny the next. Which, actually, does kind of sum up the mood of the day. The funeral itself was horrible. Rich cried, his mum cried, his dad cried, various relatives both young and old cried. His granddad was a little wizened figure in the front row, stooped and shaking with grief. And me, Cass, Donna, Ashley and even Jack and Ollie all cried because it was horrible seeing Rich so upset.

Like, there was a good turn-out and the vicar did a nice eulogy. He'd known Nanny Blue pretty well cos she'd gone to his church (although Rich told us she only went for the social side and was ninety-eight per cent certain she didn't believe). Rich said a few words about her, which was so moving I thought my head would explode with the effort of crying quietly. He'd obviously loved her so much. My heart ached for him that she was gone.

So, yeah, it went well. But in the end it was still our friend saying goodbye to his nan, whose decomposing body was in a wooden box at the end of the church.

But, strangely, the wake afterwards was completely different. It was quiet to begin with, but there was soon almost a party atmosphere, with people drinking to Nanny Blue and talking about their happy memories of her. It was a celebration of her life, I guess. Even Rich seemed to enjoy it, although every now and then he'd have to disappear to some quiet corner to compose himself.

But that was a bit later. We'd arrived at the pub, or 'sixteenth-century coaching inn' as the sign on our table said, before Rich and his family, cos they'd gone to the family-only cremation ceremony/service/whatever you call it. We recognized a few of Rich's extended family, but we didn't really know anyone else. It felt wrong to be there without him, like we were gate-crashing, and I don't know about the others but I wanted to hang on to their clothes like a kid hangs on to his mum the first day of big school.

As we sat down I got a text from Joe:

> Sorry bout the other night babe. I'm free next Thurs

& Fri – come & see me?
Will give u undivided
attention . . . x

I smiled to myself, suppressing a little squeal of glee. That was half term sorted, then. A few days in Devon, then two days with Joe. Perfect. Without saying anything to the others, I put my phone away to reply later. Even I knew that now wasn't the time or place to be texting.

'Poor Rich,' said Ash, voicing what we were all thinking. 'What he must be going through.'

'And his mum,' added Jack, who was carefully tearing the order of service into strips.

I sighed. 'It'll happen to us all.' And then: 'What?' as Donna started smirking into her Diet Coke. But I was already biting my cheeks trying not to smile.

Ash shook her head. 'You're sick, the pair of you.'

'Uh-huh, so why are you smiling then?' asked Cass, whose own mouth was turning up at the edges.

And then we were all silently vibrating with laughter, looking down at the table so we wouldn't catch anyone's eye.

'Oh God, we're so going to hell,' squeaked Cass.

'I know,' I said, rushing to get the words out before another wave of hysteria hit me. 'What kind of freak laughs at a wake?'

'It's just the tension,' came a voice from beside us. Rich. That shut us up. We hadn't seen him come in.

'Oh, mate . . . Look, we didn't mean . . .' Jack was distraught, but Rich stopped him.

'Don't worry about it. Honestly.' He sat down and put a bottle of Champagne, or fizzy wine anyway, on the table. 'So . . .' He twisted the cork. 'I want to drink to Nanny Blue.' He ceremonially popped the cork and poured seven small glasses. 'To my nan,' he said, holding his glass high then downing it in one. It was a bit weird, to be honest. Like something someone our parents' age would do. The rest of us exchanged worried looks. 'Don't worry,' he said, laughing. 'I'm not going to get pissed. Or high.' He shrugged. 'She used to propose a toast every time she had a drink. It didn't have to be anything big. She'd drink to, like, a sunny day, or more *Fawlty Towers* repeats on G.O.L.D., or whatever . . . It was just one of her things.'

Cass held her glass up – 'To Nanny Blue!' – and we all did the same.

'How's your granddad doing?' asked Ollie, after we'd all been up to the buffet to get our plates of quiche and pasta salad.

Rich shrugged. 'Dunno.'

'D'you think you'll become closer and stuff, now your nan's gone?' asked Donna.

Rich shook his head. 'No way. I don't see why I should start being nice to him now, when he's barely said a civil word to me. And he was always horrible to Nan.' We followed his gaze as he looked over at his granddad, who cut a pretty pathetic figure, sitting on his own and crying into his Guinness.

'Don't feel sorry for him,' said Rich, seeing the expression on my face. 'Why do you think no one's sitting with him, even at his wife's funeral?'

Cass's brow creased with the effort of not sympathizing with the old man. 'How did he and your nan meet?'

'She was his secretary. He's a few years older than her . . . than she was,' he corrected himself. 'She says . . . *said* he was charming and wealthy and swept her off her feet and shit . . . The charm certainly didn't last long, though. God knows why she stayed with the bastard.'

As if he could hear us, his granddad got to his feet and started tottering over to us, swaying and stumbling and obviously hammered. 'Great,' muttered Rich.

'All right, poof?' said his granddad, slapping a gnarly hand on Rich's shoulder. 'Bit of a nerve, bringing your boyfriend.' He fixed rheumy eyes on Ollie, who was sitting next to Rich.

'He's not my boyfriend, Granddad,' said Rich, through gritted teeth, his eyes down.

'Yeah yeah, I believe you, thousands wouldn't.' And with that he tottered off in the direction of the toilets.

Rich looked at Ollie. 'Sorry, mate.'

He shrugged. 'Don't worry about it.' But you could tell he was a bit shaken. We all were.

Rich tried to laugh it off. 'Look, just ignore him. He's a disgusting old bigot, and he's drunk. My mum told me about this one time . . .' And he started telling us stories about what his granddad used to get up to when he was drunk, most of which ended up with the proverbial custard pie in his granddad's face and were so outrageous we couldn't help laughing. I caught Cass's eye and she gave me a sideways smile. Rich somehow always managed to avoid getting into conversations about his sexuality. He'd once told Donna that he wasn't into confessionals. He is what he is, and he doesn't feel the need to label it. Which, as Donna said at the time, was just a typically Rich way of saying it's none of your business. And, actually, if I'm honest, lovely as Rich is, I think he likes being a bit of a man of mystery.

As the afternoon went on the atmosphere got more relaxed, and we slowly split off into separate groups. Rich, Cass and Jack got talking to Rich's parents, while Ashley and Donna got hit on by a couple of sleazes who were at least forty – I don't even think they were part of the funeral party. The poor deluded men thought their luck was in. You could see them exchanging *wahey!* looks. As if. Ash and Donna were loving it, hamming it up all wide-eyed and simpering. Which left me and Ollie, sitting at our now empty table doing cake taste-tests. 'Mmm, yah . . . yah . . .' said Ollie earnestly, screwing his eyes up in concentration as he moved fondant fancy around his mouth like a cow chewing the cud. 'I'm getting sugar, and modified maize starch . . . and, yes, a definite hint of humectants.'

Giggling, I took a nibble of a plastic-looking Victoria sponge. Trying to match Ollie's serious face – how did he do it without creasing up? – I nodded vigorously. 'Oh yes. Mmm, yes, now you see this is very good. Definite emulsifier here, and . . . yes, it is, it's raising agents. Definitely raising agents.'

Ollie pinched a piece of cake from my plate. 'Actually, that looks all right.'

I watched him put it in his mouth. 'Well?'

He moaned and rolled his eyes in mock ecstasy. ''S'goooorgeous.' He grinned through cheekfuls of cheapo sponge.

'You can't beat rubbish cake,' I agreed, choosing a mini chocolate slice from the selection plate Ollie had made up.

He looked around. 'Weird that everyone seems so happy.'

I nodded. 'I know. I expected everyone to be quiet and sombre. Like, murmured conversations and lots of dabbing of eyes with lace hankies.'

Ollie laughed. 'Right, cos you always carry a lace hanky with you.'

'I do actually,' I replied, primly. 'I keep it in a pocket in my bloomers.'

'Don't, you'll drive me wild with desire,' he said, brushing his hands together to get rid of the crumbs.

'Bloomers your thing, are they?'

He gave me a pouty-mouth phwoooar, then said, 'Talking of which, how's it going with Joe?'

I smiled. 'Yeah, all right. I'm going to stay with him next week.' I hoped. I felt a little clutch of fear that I'd jinxed it just by mentioning it.

'Wicked . . . But you are coming to Devon, right?'

'Right. I'm seeing Joe after.'

'Cool.'

We sat in companionable silence for a minute, eating cake and people-watching, then Ollie said, 'Is this your first funeral?'

I nodded. 'You?'

'Well, I went to my own brother's when I was like a week old, but obviously I don't remember that.'

I spun round from my position watching the back of the room. 'Your brother?'

He looked at me. 'Yeah. I had a twin, Zac. He lived for less than a day. Something about not having grown enough in the womb . . . I don't really know.'

I was astonished. 'Ollie, how come I didn't know that?'

He shrugged. 'It's not something I advertise. No big deal, though. It's not like I miss him.'

'Do the others know?'

Ollie smiled. 'Why, you like having inside info?'

'No! That's not what I meant.' I blushed furiously.

'Flower, I was kidding. Aw, look at you, all flustered!' He stroked my cheek, then leant back in his chair and started looking around the room again. 'To be honest, I don't know if the others know. If they do it'll only be because it came up in conversation.'

I could hardly get my head round it. 'Your poor parents,' I said. 'I can't believe I never knew. Do they talk about him?'

'Yeah, it's not a taboo subject or anything, and there are photos of him. We were identical.' He swallowed and looked down. It obviously still meant something to him.

'It must be strange to think you shared a womb with someone.'

Ollie nodded. 'Sometimes I even have a sense that

I remember him. It's hard to describe . . . it's nothing concrete, just a feeling.'

'Wow.' I looked at him, not really knowing what to say, and he smiled.

'It's fine. C'mon, let's not get morose at a funeral.' He rolled his eyes. '*Such* a cliché.'

Suddenly I noticed a pretty girl about our age eyeing Ollie up from a nearby table. I nudged him. 'Hey, someone's got their eye on you.' I glanced in the girl's direction.

Ollie raised his eyebrows. 'Oh yeah.' He turned back to me. 'A woman of taste, obviously.'

'Go and talk to her,' I said. 'Don't stay here on my account.'

He shook his head. 'Nah, I'm fine.' He smiled. 'I'm OK here.'

11

It was Devon Day.

'Here they are!' Cass waved as Jack's clapped-out blue Fiesta came into view at the top of her road. He beeped a fanfare and the four of us all waved like loons, squealing and generally getting over-excited. It was the perfect day for a road trip. Painfully blue sky, not too cold, and the trees like an advert for autumn. And I'd spoken to Joe the night before. Happy days.

The boys unfolded themselves from the car and we all spent a joyful few seconds jumping up and down and hugging. Jack tried his best to grab me, Ash, Donna and Cass in a sort of one-man group hug, until Rich and Ollie joined him and we were all smooshed together in a big bundle of happy.

Donna was the first to extricate herself. She rubbed her hands together. 'Right, when you've all finished penetrating each other, we should make a move.'

Within seconds Cass had a road map unfolded on the bonnet of her brother's car. She beckoned everyone over. 'OK, Jack and I'll drive till here.' She pointed at a services near Bournemouth. 'Then we'll stop for lunch and Donna and Rich can drive the rest of the way.' She looked sternly at me, Ashley and Ollie. 'And you three are making dinner tonight due to your slackness in not learning to drive in time for this trip.'

We piled into the cars, boys in one, girls in the other. Ash leant out of her window and shouted at the boys' car. 'Oi, you lot. No racing, OK? It's lame. And we'd win.' She pointedly looked Jack's little car up and down. He flicked her some cheerful Vs, and we were off.

Cass was a good driver, as careful as you'd expect from Little Miss List-Maker, but pretty confident too. I was a bit in awe. I knew I should learn to drive, but frankly I was scared of having the potential to kill someone without meaning to. Not that I'd ever mean to, but you know what I mean. Anyway, I lucked out and got to sit in the front passenger seat. It was that kind of day. I flicked through the CDs in the glove compartment. Cass had obviously turfed out her brother's and brought her own in.

'Right, we've got *Glee Season One* . . .' Retching from Ashley. 'Or there's Adele, Marina and the Diamonds, Ellie Goulding, Rihanna or . . . Oh my God . . .' I slowly turned to face Cass. 'Cassandra, really. Michael Bublé?' Uproar in the car. Cass went scarlet.

'Oh my God, it's totally my mum's!' she protested. 'I've no idea how it got in there!'

'I've never heard such a girlie bunch of music in my life,' said Ash. 'But I could handle a bit of Rihanna – not "Umbrella", though.'

It was perfect. There isn't much that can lift the soul like driving to Devon with your best friends and bellowing 'Cheers (Drink to That)' with props to whoever can do the best Bajan accent. Life-affirming, that's what it was.

After nearly an hour of singing and throwing of seat-bound R&B shapes, we gradually fell silent, the movement of the car lulling us. I relaxed and gazed out of the window. I was like the pinnacle of contented. Three more days, and I'd be with Joe again. I couldn't wait. Smiling to myself, I started writing a quick text.

> On way to Devon. See u in
> few days 4 fun n
> debauchery xx

'Who're you texting?' asked Cass. She must have excellent peripheral vision – I never saw her eyes leave the road for a second.

I didn't look up from my phone. 'Just Joe.' She nodded slightly but didn't say anything. She was concentrating on a massive lorry in front of us that was indicating to move into our lane. 'God, I so can't wait to see him,' I continued. 'It feels like ages since we saw each other.'

'It *has* been ages,' said Cass. 'I don't know how you do it. I miss Adam if I don't see him, like, every two days, let alone for weeks on end.'

OK. Quite annoying. 'Yeah well, ours is a different kind of relationship,' I said, doing my best to keep my tone even. 'Joe lives in London, I live in Brighton . . . We were never going to see each other every day.'

Cass took her hand off the steering wheel so she could pat my leg. 'Poor old Sar Bear.'

'Nah, it's OK,' I said. 'When we do get together it's like all the other times we could have been together are condensed into –' I rolled my eyes and put on a cheesy advert voice – 'über sex.'

Cass grinned. 'Ew, Sarah. TMI, lady.'

I giggled. It was still a novelty to even be in the position of having too much information. I craned round to look at the back seats. Ash and Donna were fast asleep, Ashley's head on Donna's shoulder, drool inching out of the side of her mouth. Donna's head was flung back, her mouth hanging open like she was catching flies. I tapped Cass's hand and spoke through the side of my mouth. 'Sleeping beauties, six o'clock.' She looked in her rear-view mirror and giggled.

'Aw, bless 'em. Quick, take a photo.' But I was already holding up my phone. Definitely one for Facebook.

We sped along in companionable silence for a few more minutes. Then Cass said, 'Actually, I haven't seen Adam for a few days. He's been really busy at work.'

It was my turn to pat her leg. It was stupid to get annoyed with her. She had it tough with him – we should be supporting each other. 'Cass . . .' I began, grateful that she had to keep her eyes on the road. 'Do you ever . . . I dunno . . . like, wonder whether you're doing the right thing staying with Adam? I'm only asking cos, y'know, me and Joe . . .'

'All the time,' she said, without hesitation.

'So . . . why do you?' I asked.

She pulled at her bottom lip. 'Cos I would die if we broke up.'

I studied her face to see if she was purposely being over-dramatic, but her expression hadn't changed. 'Wow.'

She smiled briefly. 'I know.'

I ran my hand through my hair. 'I sometimes wonder. About Joe, I mean . . . Like, he told that Mimi girl that I was a virgin before we did it . . . and other stuff.'

It was the first time I'd told anyone, but Cass didn't seem overly bothered, although I couldn't see the expression on her face. 'That was nice of him,' she said wryly. 'What did he say when you brought him up on it?'

'Well . . . There's a chance I may have just let it go,' I mumbled.

Cass shot me a look. 'Sarah, hon, Adam has his faults – I know you lot think that I don't know, but, believe me, I do. But I also know he'd never tell another girl about our sex life.'

'Yeah, but. Joe and Mimi are friends. Friends talk to each other.' But even as I said it I thought: this is exactly what Cass does. She stands up for Adam when it's blatantly obvious to everyone that he's been a total dickwad.

Cass looked sceptical. 'Some friend she is.' And I had to agree with her. I decided I'd confront Joe when I saw him. He needed to know the way his so-called friend had spoken to me, and that I wasn't comfortable with him revealing my private stuff. We would discuss it like adults and move on. I couldn't let little things like this fester if we had any kind of a future together.

'I guess me and Joe'll be living together by the time we've been a couple as long as you and Adam have,' I mused. I had to bite my cheek to stop myself grinning like an idiot.

'Ooh, so you are a couple now?' said Cass. 'When did THAT happen?'

'Uh, well . . . *couple*'s just a word,' I backtracked. 'It's not like he *announced* it or anything.'

Cass raised her eyebrows — sceptically? — and we fell into silence again.

After a few minutes I said, 'Cass, you won't tell the others . . .'

She interrupted me. 'Course not. Don't be silly.'

We got to the services before the boys. Not that it was a race or anything — that would be immature — but we legged it into the building, giggling like idiots, scrabbling to look settled at a table before they arrived. We needn't have bothered. They were a good fifteen minutes behind us, sauntering in as if they couldn't care less. Yeah, right. Ashley raised an eyebrow and Jack held up his hand. 'Before you say anything, we had to stop for petrol.'

Cass smiled smugly as she flicked through her *Lonely Planet Guide to Devon and Cornwall*. 'Should have filled up before we left, like I did.'

'Mi mi mi mi mi mi mi,' mocked Rich, making yack-yack movements with his hands. Cass didn't look up from her book, but I could see her cheekbones rise as she smiled.

'Anyway,' I said, rubbing my hands together. 'I'm starving . . .'

As was everyone else, although it took a good ten

minutes of earnest discussion for everyone to decide what they wanted. Ollie and I were put in charge of the Burger King run.

'D'you think they're going to make us work all week to make up for not being able to do a driving shift?' I asked him as we waited in the queue.

He looked glum. 'Probably. We'll be like Cinderella, up before dawn to sweep out the fireplaces.'

'And when exactly was the last time you swept anything?' I said, going for an Ashley-style raised eyebrow.

'Exactly. I'll be rubbish at it.' He shook his head sorrowfully. 'Looks like you're on sweeping duty, McSarey.'

I laughed. 'Silly Ollie.'

He tilted his head in acknowledgement then nodded at the server. 'Look lively, we're next.'

The second half of the journey was not so much fun. An accident meant we were stuck in traffic for hours, so when we at last got to the youth hostel it was late and we were stiff, tired and grouchy. Donna got pissed off with Cass for bossing everyone around, Ash snapped at Jack for practising his cricket bowling with an invisible ball instead of joining in an argument about bedrooms, and Rich did a huge, exaggerated yawn when I mentioned in passing that

I was waiting for a text from Joe. And all this while we were still checking in.

'OH I DO LIKE TO BE BESIDE THE SEA-SIDE!' a stadium-loud gravelly voice boomed behind us.

We all spun round to find Ollie sliding to his knees, strumming an air guitar in joke classic-rock style. Of course. Such an exhibitionist.

'Thank you,' he said, taking a little bow. 'Now can I respectfully request that we all get a freaking grip? We're on holiday, people.' He grabbed Donna's sleeve with one hand and Cass's arm with the other and pushed them together. 'Now kiss and make up, quick, so we can all go and get pissed.'

Rich licked his lips disgustingly. 'Mmm-*mm*, hot lesbo action.'

Donna pretended to kick him. 'Right, cos that's like your total dream fantasy.'

Rich closed his eyes in an *ask me no questions I'll tell you no lies* smirk, and we all trooped off to the boys' room.

Donna sloshed vodka and then Coke into the mugs we'd borrowed from the hostel kitchen. We were sitting on the floor leaning against the room's two metal bunk beds, the boys in a row opposite me, Ash, Donna and Cass. It was pretty uncomfortable, but the alternative was sitting on the top bunks, where there wasn't anywhere to put our drinks. So floor it was.

'Who's up for a quick game of *Have You Ever?* then?' Donna asked, as she licked the foam that had spilled down the side of her cup. Groans all round, but everyone agreed. Me and Cass shared a look. We'd talked about this before. If an idea came from Donna, Ashley or the boys, it was good. Like, sometimes it might be ironic-good (*Have You Ever?* definitely fell into this category), but it was always good. If we'd come up with the current plan, it'd have been laughed down as lame. I smiled at her and shrugged. I was actually happy to play the game. Now I had a . . . boyfriend? Now I had Joe, anyway, I had some sexual past to draw on. One time we'd played – we'd been in Year Eleven, I think – I'd caused much hilarity when I'd made some comment about sperm being yellow. I couldn't remember why I thought it was yellow, or even why the subject had come up, but the memory made me go bright red with retrospective shame. Like, when you know something, the idea of not knowing it is instantly unthinkable. If I'd heard someone tell me that spunk was yellow now, I'd have gone hot and cold with embarrassment for them.

Donna tapped her lips with a fingertip. 'Who wants to start?' She narrowed her eyes and scanned each of us in turn.

Finally Ollie said, 'Go on then, I've got one.'

Donna swept her palm across the rectangle of blue institutional carpet that was the space between us. 'The floor is yours.'

He tapped his fingers against the side of his mug for a second. 'Have you ever . . .' He paused for dramatic effect. 'Been in love?'

I actually blinked with surprise. I'd been expecting something sexual: have you ever done it in public, or have you ever farted while having oral sex (a particularly lovely one to Ashley from Donna last time we played the game, to which Ash genteely answered, 'Ugh, no way, you skanky bitch'). Rich slung his arm across Ollie's shoulders and held an imaginary microphone in front of his face. 'So when exactly was it that you decided to become a woman?'

Ollie shrugged him off. 'Piss off. Does it always have to be about shagging?' He was laughing, but it had a bit of an edge.

Rich, Donna and Ashley looked at each other. 'Yes!' They high-fived each other.

'I agree with Ollie, for what it's worth,' said Jack mildly.

Ollie shook his hand. 'Thanks, man.'

'Go on then.' Ashley stretched her leg and tapped Jack's foot with her own. 'What's your answer? Have you ever been in love?'

He smiled lopsidedly. 'I have, actually.'

That got everyone's attention. 'No way!' said Ash. 'Who?'

'Leanne Hannigan.'

Rich scrunched his forehead. 'Why do I know that name?'

Cass clicked her fingers at him. 'C'mon: Leanne Hannigan. Twin sister called Carrie-Anne? Wet herself in PE once?'

Rich smiled as realization dawned. 'God, yeah. Leanne Hannigan.' Then he frowned. 'But sod off – that was in primary school. We were, like, five years old. That doesn't count.'

'Yeah it does,' said Jack. 'I was completely in love with her. She lived on our road and she'd play football with me after school. She was pretty good.'

'Aw, that's so sweet,' Cass cooed, her head on one side. 'So what happened?'

'Her family moved away. I was gutted when she left.' He shrugged and smiled.

Ollie patted his shoulder. 'Tough, mate. Tough.'

'What about you, Olster?' Donna pulled up the ankle of her jeans to scratch an insect bite, then sat with her knees bent and her legs apart like a boy. I saw Jack glance at her crotch then look away quickly.

Ollie put his hands behind his head and stretched out his legs. 'You know me. I'm not one for the steady girlfriend.'

'Or indeed any girlfriend,' said Ashley drily. 'Heart-breaker of Woodside High, you are.'

'I'm bloody not!' said Ollie indignantly. 'Name one heart I've broken.' Ash demurred grudgingly. He was right. Everyone loved him. It was like if you had sex with Ollie it was part of being his friend. He treated everyone exactly the same, and that never changed no matter what you did together. Or at least that's how it seemed to me, from the outside. None of us had ever slept with him – that would have been too weird. He and Donna had snogged each other once, years ago, but that was kids' stuff.

'I've never been in love. Not even close,' said Donna, as if she'd just remembered that incident too. She didn't look bothered by her lack of love. I didn't understand how she could fancy someone enough to have sex with them, and not fall in love with them just a little bit.

Ashley shook her head. 'Me neither. But then look at me . . .' She ran the back of her hand up and down her body as if she was fanning herself.

'What?' Rich grinned. 'Too "alternative" to fall in love?'

'Piss off, that's not what I meant.'

Rich blew her a kiss and she picked an imaginary bogey and flicked it at him in return. He pretended to catch it in his mouth. 'Mmm, meaty.'

Sometimes I think it's a good thing that Rich is in the closet.

'I've been in love. Still am,' said Cass, after the laughter and groans of disgust had died down. 'But you knew that already.'

'Ah yes, the delectable Adam,' said Donna into her mug, before taking a few gulps. Cass shot her a hurt look but didn't rise to it. There was a pause in the conversation.

'What about you, Sar?' said Rich. 'You're very quiet over there.'

I'd been pondering what to say. I was in love with Joe, no doubt about it, but it seemed too important to reveal in a game. Like to say it would make it less real. And anyway, I didn't want the others to take the piss or think I was being hasty or whatever. Yes, it was soon to be feeling this strongly, but when you know you know.

'Speak for yourself,' I shot back to give myself more time. 'I notice you haven't answered the question yet.'

He rubbed his back where it'd been pressed against the cold metal of the bunk bed. 'Pass.'

'You're not allowed to pass,' sniped Cass.

'Who says? The rule book?' said Rich reasonably. 'Sorry, I'm not answering this one.' And because it was Rich, and because we were being gentle with him cos of his nan, we let it go. I wished I'd thought of passing. I couldn't now, or they'd think I was copying him.

'C'mon, McSarey, spill the beans.' Ollie waggled his eyebrows at me.

'The answer is no,' I said, looking into my glass to avoid making eye contact with anyone. 'I've never been in love.' I'd expected everyone to call me on it, but they didn't.

'OK, my turn,' said Ash, rubbing her hands together. 'Have you ever . . . had a sex dream about a teacher?'

Back in the girls' room a couple of hours later I lay on my top bunk (result!) and texted Joe. He hadn't replied to my earlier message, but I knew he was working a double shift at the bar.

'You're so texting Joe.' Cass's voice came floating up from the bottom bunk.

'No sexting in communal spaces, thanks very much,' added Ashley. 'Très bad form.'

'As if.' But I wasn't really listening to them. I was deciding whether writing 'tonite' instead of 'tonight' would put Joe off or make me seem relaxed and easy-going. But then the automatic spell check changed it to 'tonight' anyway and I decided it was massively lame to deliberately misspell a spell-checked word.

'How's it going, babes?' asked Donna. 'You're see-ing him on Thursday, right?'

I pressed Send and clicked the button that switched off the screen. I turned on to my side, the bed springs twanging and creaking beneath me. I could feel the pupils of my eyes expanding in the darkness. 'Yeah. It's good, thanks . . . he's good.'

'Ooooh!' squealed Ash. 'You lurve him.'

I smiled. 'He is rather lovely. I can't wait to see him . . . It'd better work this time. We have just the worst luck – something always seems to come up and he has to cancel. I suppose that's what you get for having a boyfriend –' I giggled slightly at the word – 'who's a student. He works, he has essay deadlines, all that stuff . . . We just have different stuff going on, you know? But, like, give it ten months and I'll be a stu-dent too. We just have to work through this first, difficult bit. We'll get there.' I stopped to draw breath, but before I could continue Ashley suddenly gasped and changed the subject, making my stomach con-strict. Had I been going on about Joe? I really hadn't! And Donna shouldn't have asked if she didn't want to know the answer. I sighed to myself. Anyway, moving on . . .

'Oh my God, what was with Rich and refusing to say if he'd ever been in love?' said Ash.

'I know! Do you think it's cos he's in love with . . .'

Cass lowered her voice to a scandalized whisper. 'A boy?' We giggled vaguely hysterically, me included. This was so not something we were supposed to talk about. Even among ourselves we rarely brought it up, although I didn't really know why. I think it was because Rich wouldn't talk about it, so as his friends we had to assume he was straight, even though we all thought he wasn't. None of us wanted to be the first to out him, basically, in case we were wrong after all.

'Or maybe he's in love with one of us?' I said, earnestly. 'He did eat one of your bogeys, Ash. Only someone who really loved you could do that.'

'Oh man, you're sick. He's so not my type.'

'Well, it's good to know you draw the line somewhere,' said Donna. 'Even if it is at people who don't actually fancy girls.'

'You don't know that,' said Cass, seriously. 'He could be bisexual.'

Donna suddenly sat up, making the whole bunk wobble. 'Oh my God, I've just thought of something. Like, he and Jack have been best friends forever. Jack hasn't got a girlfriend . . .'

'Shit, you're right. They're probably humping away next door as we speak.' Ash tried to keep her tone dry, but she was getting as over-excited as the rest of us.

'Ugh, don't,' said Cass. 'Poor Ollie.'

I giggled. I know everyone thought I was sweet and gullible, but really. Cass was way worse. 'You do know they're not actually having sex, right?'

'Piss off.' But I could hear the smile in her voice. 'It is quite sad though, when you think about it,' she went on. 'Rich feeling he has to hide his love.'

I rolled my eyes in the dark. 'Yeah. Either that or he just wanted to seem mysterious and interesting.'

'Yeah, no, that's a good point,' said Ash. 'That's totally the kind of thing he'd do.'

And with that the conversation petered out and we fell asleep.

'Wake up, time to eat!'

I peered over the edge of my bed to find the source of the disgustingly chirpy voice and rhythmical thumping. It was Donna doing star jumps. Of course.

'What time is it?' I croaked. I ran my tongue over my teeth. I'd have killed for a glass of water.

'Just gone nine.' Donna's voice shook as she contin-ued her morning exercises. She looked amazing, and slightly terrifying. Mad hair all over the place, mascara smudges down her cheeks, and un-tethered boobs bouncing crazily beneath her Snoopy pyjama top.

'What the hell are you doing, woman?' groaned Ashley from underneath her covers. 'It's the crack of dawn.'

Donna changed to a kind of leap-up-and-down-while-punching-the-air-with-alternate-fists thing. Probably not its official title, but I'd rather have chewed my arm off than go to an exercise class. Coordination and me are not best friends. I once tripped over my own shadow. (Not a joke. The scar on my knee proves it.)

'I'm getting energized,' she panted, moving on to lunges. 'And it's late. They stop serving breakfast in, like, twenty minutes.' She sat on the edge of her bed, breathing hard.

'I'll come with you. I'm starving,' I said, climbing down from my bunk, the ladder creaking metallically.

She gave me a breathless thumbs-up. 'Nice one.'

In the end we all trooped downstairs to eat. Cass and Donna had refused to go until they'd showered and done their make-up, so by the time we made it to the dining room we had to do some serious sweet-talking to get them to serve us. Well, Cass and Donna did the sweet-talking. They did, after all, look the most respectable. The rest of us looked like dehydrated scarecrows in pyjamas. Surprisingly the boys were already there, fully dressed and tucking into sausage, egg and beans. Rich waved us over with his fork.

'Just what I like, a man waving his sausage at me first thing in the morning.' Ash flopped down in the chair next to him and stole a chip from his plate. 'Since when were these acceptable food for breakfast?'

'Get your bloody own,' he griped. 'And chips are the food of champions. Everyone knows that.'

'Whatever.' A youngish man with blond dreadlocks came to take our order. 'I'll have what they're having,' said Ash, accepting Rich's ironic high-five graciously.

We all ordered then leant back in our chairs contentedly. No parents, no deadlines, no responsibility. It was a good feeling.

'So what are we doing today?' asked Cass, whipping her notebook from her sleeve like an OCD magician. 'What? It's useful!' she said over our jeers.

Jack stroked her hair. 'You're gonna make someone an excellent wife one day . . .' He waved his hand airily. 'Organizing dinner parties and what not.' He smiled sheepishly and twiddled his fork. Like his parents ever had dinner parties.

Cass smiled as she wrote something at the top of the page and underlined it. 'I think you'll find, young Jack, that my organizational skills will be invaluable when I become Prime Minister.'

'Right on, sister,' I said, doing a quick air-punch. Ash and Donna joined in with some whoops, and Cass beamed, her cheeks turning a becoming pink.

She was so rarely the centre of attention, bless her, but she wasn't even joking – not much, anyway – about the Prime Minister thing. Beneath the puppy-dog exterior lay ambition of steel. The girl had a twenty-year plan, for God's sake. I barely had a one-week plan, and we know what – or who – that centred on.

And, as if by magic, my mobile chirped, making a manic *brrr* noise as it vibrated against the plastic table top. 'Ahem, très rude,' said Ash, giving it a pointed stare.

'Sorry, sorry. I was just waiting for this. I'll put it away in a sec.' I quickly tapped in my passcode and the text came up in full:

> Sounds good. Don't get
> too drunk. See you in
> couple days x

Most of the time with texts from Joe I had to scroll up to remind myself exactly what he was replying to. There were way more texts from me to him than from him to me. But that was boys for you. I was itching to text back, but I put the phone in my pocket and concentrated on demolishing the huge plate of food that had just been put in front of me.

We never did get round to making Cass's list. Jack got everyone into the idea of playing volleyball on the beach. It was me, Rich and Ash against Donna, Cass and Ollie. Jack was the ref cos it wouldn't be fair on the other team if he played. He drew a line in the sand with a stick.

'Right, this is the net. Your aim is to get the ball to touch the ground on the other side. We'll play best of three.' He held the ball we'd borrowed from the hostel over the line and chucked it up in the air. If he'd had a whistle, he'd totally have given it a sharp blast.

Rich and Cass both leapt for the ball, with Rich – who's a good five inches taller than Cass – bashing it over the 'net'. Cass threw herself after it, managing to hit it back. I went for it, but it slipped through my hands. One–nil to them.

'Nice one, Sarah,' sniped Rich, scooping up the ball and shooting me evils. I didn't mind. He and Cass both turn into tyrants when it comes to competition. They'll do pretty much anything to win – including cheat. It's not worth getting worked up about.

Ash dug her elbow into Rich's side. 'Cheer up, Venus Williams, it's only a game.'

He looked at her scathingly. 'Hello? Venus Williams is tennis?'

Me, Ash and Ollie exchanged grins. How to rile Rich in one easy step.

Jack put his hand out for the ball. 'Right. One–nil to Cass, Donna and Ollie. Nice work, Cassie.'

She smiled at him, showing her dimples. 'Cheers, Jack.' But his head was back in the game. Sport is a v. serious business for our Jack.

'Ready?'

We nodded, all leaping from foot to foot and puffing extravagantly, except Rich and Cass who were doing it for real, and he chucked the ball into play again.

'IT'S MINE!' screamed Ash, and she sent it barrelling at a million miles an hour into the opposing side.

But Ollie was on it. 'AAAGGGGHHHH!' He did a double-fist punch under the ball, and it spiralled way up into the sky, seemed to hover in mid-air for a second *à la* Wile E. Coyote before he falls into the canyon, then came whizzing back down to earth, landing a millimetre on the wrong side of the line. He looked round at us, a lopsided grin on his face. 'Bugger. What are the chances?' We all fell about laughing, although obviously Cass wasn't amused. Ollie put his arm round her. 'Sorry, babes. I'll do better next time.' She scowled, but not really. It's kind of impossible to be cross with Ollie for long.

And so it went on. We won, but only just. Rich was a good winner, thumping Cass on the back and telling her it was a close thing and we'd been lucky really, which was true. It'd been great. Bright and gusty and fun, and, as if it had been waiting for us to finish our game, the temperature dropped and the sky started turning grey just as we trooped back to the hostel for lunch. A perfect morning.

After a distinctly non-Seven-Go-To-Devon-y lunch of limp sandwiches and Tesco Value crisps, everyone decided they were gagging to play the slot machines on the seafront. Needless to say, it wasn't me or Cass who suggested it, although Cass seemed enthusiastic enough. I couldn't think of anything more depressing, so I stayed behind to sit in the hostel lounge, drink tea and read magazines in front of the fire. At the last minute Ash changed her mind about going, making some joke about going for a swim instead. So the rest skipped off to waste their money, leaving me to an old *Woman & Home* magazine, and Ash to annoying me. I could feel her presence in the next chair like an itch. I knew she wanted something before she even opened her mouth.

'Sarah?'

I sighed. 'Hmm?'

'Can I ask a reeeeally big favour?'

Another, bigger sigh. 'What?'

'Will you come swimming with me? In the sea?'

My mouth dropped open. She'd been serious about that? 'No, freako, funnily enough, I won't.' I pointedly turned back to my magazine.

'Oh come on, please,' wheedled Ashley. 'Don't be a wuss. It'll be exhilarating.'

I shook my head. 'No way. I'm not bloody swimming in the sea in late October. Anyway, I haven't brought my swimming costume. Obviously.'

'Well, just come with me then. Please, Sar.' She looked at me beseechingly.

I threw down my book. 'Bloody hell.'

She clapped her hands. 'Yay! Thanks, babes.' I harrumphed, but got my coat and followed her out of the door.

'Why would you even want to do this?' I asked as we stumbled back down the path to the beach. 'It's freezing. And we live in Brighton, for God's sake. Does that not have enough sea for you?'

Ash shrugged happily. She was skipping along beside me like a little kid. 'I've just always wanted to do it. When I was little I saw something on telly about those people who go swimming in, like, arctic temperatures and, I dunno, it just looked amazing . . . Like –' She stopped skipping to grasp for the right words – 'like they were cheating nature. And Brighton's not special enough for that.'

I shoved my hands into my pockets grumpily. 'It's not bloody cheating nature . . . it's just mental. Why d'you want me there, anyway?'

Ash linked her arm through mine. 'Dunno. Just

suddenly wanted someone to mark the occasion. C'mon, Sar, this is one of my ten things to do before I die. Be happy for me.'

Surprised, I turned to her. 'You've got an actual list?' Ash nodded. 'What else is on it?'

Without pause, Ash reeled them off. 'Round-the-world trip, perform at Glastonbury, write novel, have sex with girl, get married, have children, have general anaesthetic, fly plane, learn to cook.'

I mulled over those for a minute. Sex with a girl? Interesting. General anaesthetic? Weird, but I could sort of see her thinking. I rubbed my eye. 'You want to get married and have children?'

Ash smirked. 'I knew you'd pick up on that.' Her expression was light, but her mouth was tense. This list business was obviously no joke, then. I altered my expression accordingly.

'I can't help what I want, can I?' she said. We walked in silence for a few seconds. 'It's like . . .' She stopped. 'Do you believe in God?'

I shrugged. 'Dunno. I suppose so.'

'Well, I've thought about it a lot,' she said. 'It'd be nice to believe in heaven and all that, but I don't. I can't . . . It's the same with the marriage-and-children thing. I'd rather not want them, but I do.'

I smiled at her. 'Blimey, you've really thought this through.'

She raised an eyebrow. "'Blimey'"?'

'Piss off.'

Ash chuckled and resumed her joyful skipping, while I trudged along behind her and mulled over what I'd have on my list. I knew what'd be at number one, anyway.

'So what happens now?' I asked, as we walked across the beach. The lunchtime downpour had turned the sand heavy and dark, and the sea was metal-grey and choppy. It looked about as inviting as you'd imagine. Ash was stepping out of her jeans and pulling her jumper over her head, revealing her plain black swimming costume underneath. She jumped up and down on the spot.

'You sit here and marvel while I conquer the waves, obviously.' She shivered, laughing giddily. Her excitement was infectious. My stomach felt tense, like waiting for exam results.

'Go on, then,' I said, laughing. 'Swim like the wind!'

'WHOOOOOO!' Ash threw her arms in the air and ran into the waves, the echo of her call twisting and bobbing on the air currents. She swam hard for a few metres then turned and waved. I waved back, then laid my coat on the wet sand and sat down, putting Ashley's coat round my shoulders for warmth. There were a few surfers further along the water, but

I couldn't see any boats. I shivered. I couldn't think of anything worse than strapping myself to a surfboard and throwing myself to the freezing waves, although that's more or less what Ashley had done – minus the surfboard. The mentalist.

She was ploughing up and down parallel with the shoreline now. I could just make her out. Visibility was pretty rubbish. The horizon seemed really close, and the sea and sky kind of merged in a drizzly haze. I pulled out my ponytail elastic, tried to smooth back the hair that the wind had whipped into a tangled frenzy, and put the elastic back in, tight as I could. My gaze wandered along the shore. It took me a few seconds to find Ashley this time. She was swimming on her back now, I thought. I could just make out her arms slicing through the water. Then she stopped.

I stood up and walked to the water's edge. Was she looking this way? I waved, but she didn't wave back. Why wasn't she swimming any more? Squinting, I tried to work out what she was doing. I saw her face, small and pale above the water, and then it disappeared under the surface, before bobbing up again. Something in the angle of her head made me feel nervous, like she was struggling to keep her mouth and nose above water. Suddenly a poem we'd studied in English popped into my head. It was about a swimming man waving at onlookers on the beach. Only he wasn't waving.

I must have thought something – made some kind of decision – but I can't remember doing either of those things. My memory of it is that I just instinctively tore off Ashley's coat, waded out until the sea was deep enough and dived in. The shock of the freezing water made me gasp, but I kept thinking of something I'd read somewhere: the average person drowns in under a minute.

It felt surreal to be in the sea in my clothes, my nose full of the same salty, seaweedy smell as every seaside holiday I'd ever been on. It was like a bad dream. It was almost like I was watching myself, although the cold and the waves were real enough. The current pulled heavy at my legs, my sodden jeans weighing me down. It felt like I was dragging sandbags behind me – my legs must have been next to useless, and in fact afterwards my arms ached for days – but fear pushed me forward. As I got closer I could see Ashley's eyes wide and unseeing and her mouth twisted with pain as she fought with something under the surface while simultaneously trying to keep her mouth above water. Every time the water swelled she swallowed a mouthful and retched. Telling myself not to panic, there aren't any sharks in Devon, I swam up to her, the waves strong but not overpowering. Ash hadn't seen me, and in the few seconds it took me to reach her, the waves pulling me back slightly with each forward stroke, I quite clearly saw her give up. She closed her eyes – and I shouted – but she was already sinking beneath the swell. I lunged towards her and grabbed her shoulder. By some miracle I caught hold of the strap of her swimming costume. I yanked it and pulled her up enough so I could get my hand in her armpit, then I hauled her head above the surface.

'Ashley!' I barked, hardly recognizing my own voice. 'Open your eyes.' She did as she was told, and stared at me dully. I trod water and offered a short prayer of thanks that she was beyond fighting. It was using all my strength just to hold her up. 'It's OK. You're OK,' I shouted. 'Just roll on to your back. I'll do the rest.' She ignored me, closing her eyes again. 'NO!' I tried to shake her but the water made it impossible. It was like a nightmare. 'Ash, please, just DO IT,' I implored, whimpering with frustration and fear. I swam behind her and tried to use my natural buoyancy to push her body back on top of the water. Still she didn't respond, so I quickly pulled one hand away from where I was supporting her shoulders and yanked her hair, hard. Her head jerked, and she at last got the message, leaning her head back so the rest of her followed.

I started for shore, holding on to her with one hand and paddling with the other, dredging up memories from when I was ten and had to swim in pyjamas for my life-saving badge. I thought I should talk to her to tell her it was OK, but I didn't have the strength. She was too exhausted to do anything but comply anyway. I muttered the same words with each stroke, like a mantra to get me to shore. Less than a minute. Less than a minute. Part of me noticed that Ashley was feeling heavier and less responsive, but it almost seemed irrelevant now. Less than a minute. Less than a minute. Less than a . . .

'Sarah, I'm coming!' Jack's voice. I dared to look round. The shore was closer than I thought. I tentatively lowered my leg, ready to summon enough strength to lift it back up if the water was still too deep. I almost cried when my toe touched sand. Jack was with me in seconds. Grunting with effort, he lifted Ashley up out of the water and waded into shore. Her head lolled horribly and her hands flopped loosely by her sides. Jack dropped to his knees at the water's edge and laid her on the sand, taking a second to pull her arms and legs straight so she was flat on her back. I watched, mute with terror.

'Get my coat – and take your wet clothes off.' His voice was steady. I half crawled, half ran across the wet sand to his coat and thrust it at him. He took his phone out of a pocket and handed it to me. 'Call an ambulance.' Then he quickly rubbed Ashley down with his coat before turning it over and covering her from the waist down. I was shaking so much I dropped the phone. Swearing, I scrabbled for it then closed my eyes and concentrated on breathing in, breathing out as I pressed the Emergency Call button. When I opened my eyes Jack was bent over Ash, giving her mouth to mouth.

'An ambulance is on its way. I'll stay on the line,' said the call handler. I felt almost calm. For now at least, I was just about in control.

'He's doing CPR,' I said, in answer to the handler's question. 'He's trained. He's a lifeguard at the swimming pool.' My chest shuddered with grief and fear and pride as I watched Jack, the sweat patches spreading across his back as he breathed for our friend, forced her to stay alive.

The call handler said something. 'They say to tell you you're doing a really good job,' I told Jack. He nodded slightly. He was checking her pulse again.

There was a rushing in my head, but I could hear the waves continuing to break on to the shore, and Jack's breathing, and the call handler's occasional words.

And then Ashley convulsed, her eyes springing open, and Jack was suddenly animated. He pushed her on to her side and she retched, tears spilling as her body strained to get rid of the seawater and God knows what else. The coughing was raw and horrible, but she was breathing.

When he was sure there was no more to come, Jack carefully placed her in the recovery position. Then he sat back on his haunches, dropped his chin into his chest and cried.

I ended the 999 call. According to Jack's phone it had lasted exactly two minutes.

As the ambulance arrived I realized for the first time that I was shivering uncontrollably.

I don't remember much of what happened immediately after that. Ashley and I were both taken to hospital, me with mild hypothermia, Ashley with, well, whatever you call the after-effects of nearly drowning. Jack stayed behind to find the others. Cass told me afterwards that he broke down in tears as soon as he started telling them what had happened, and for a few awful seconds they all thought one of us had died.

When I woke up there was none of that *Where am I?* stuff you read about. I knew instantly I was in hospital. Where else could I be? But even so it felt like I'd woken in a different dimension where it was night, but not night. The people in the five other beds in the room all seemed to be asleep, but the place was bathed in a kind of half-light and weird disembodied noises punctuated the silence. A sort of low-level humming and beeping, with the occasional squeak of shoes on shiny plastic floor.

'Oh hello, you're awake.' A nurse was checking a clipboard that seemed to be attached to the foot of my bed. She came up beside me and took hold of my wrist to check my pulse. Her hand was cool and dry. I didn't want her to let go.

'What time is it?' I asked, but it came out as a husky whisper. I cleared my throat and tried again.

'Just gone three a.m.' The nurse put a cuff on my arm and pressed a button on a digital monitor. The cuff inflated, squeezing my arm. The nurse made a note of the readout. 'Your blood pressure's one hundred and one over sixty-five.' She gave me a brief but warm smile. 'That's good . . . How are you feeling?'

'Uh, OK I think,' I said, mentally checking myself over. 'Just really tired.'

The nurse bundled the cuff up with the monitor and nodded. 'Go back to sleep. Your parents are here, you can see them in the morning.'

Mum and Dad? I tried to sit up but the nurse touched my shoulder. 'Not now, Sarah. Go back to sleep. They'll be here when you wake up.' I fell back down on the sheets. Sleep was creeping up from my toes like warm water. I clenched my fists. Not the best analogy.

'Where's my friend?' I mumbled.

'Look to your right.'

I turned my head just enough to see that Ashley was in the next bed, her dark hair fanned out on her pillow, the blankets rising and falling as she slept.

'F'nn,' I said, too sleepy to move my lips.

The nurse patted my shoulder. 'You're welcome.'

The next time I woke up it was to sunlight and noise. Opening my eyes a smidgen, I tried to look around without anyone noticing. It felt like I'd been sleeping in a shop window. People were milling about and I could hear the clink of cutlery. Breakfast time. My tummy growled and I heard gentle laughter. Mum! Turning towards the sound, I saw her knees by my pillow. I huddled against them and she placed her hand on my head.

'Hi, Mum.' I was glad my face was hidden. I didn't trust myself not to burst into tears, which under the circumstances would have seemed embarrassingly melodramatic.

'Hello, darling.' Mum's voice broke, and I hugged her knees tighter.

I shifted so she could see my face. 'How long have you been sitting there?'

'Well, visiting hours started at eight.' She looked at her watch. 'And it's eight forty-two now.'

'Have they told you what happened?' An image of Ashley sinking under the water popped into my head. I swallowed and stretched my legs, flexing my toes against the stiff cotton of the sheet. Mum didn't answer, and, when I turned to her she was crying, her fist against her mouth. My dad had his arm round her – I hadn't noticed him before – and his eyes were brimming. Invisible hands squeezed my chest. Seeing my dad cry was the world flipped on its head. Like the time he'd shunted into the car in front and the driver stood in the street and yelled at him. I'd felt the same seeing my dad being told off as I did seeing him crying. It was wrong. I twisted my sheet. 'I'm sorry, Dad.'

Mum kind of snorted, her mouth twisting as it veered between laughing and crying. I knew how it felt. 'Oh, Sarah, don't be sorry. We're so . . . so proud of you.'

My dad took my hand. 'We're just thinking about what could have happened.'

I kept my eyes on the sheet, pleating it between my fingers. 'Well, don't,' I said quietly.

'I know, Sooz, you're right.' (My dad calls me Sooz. Don't ask.) 'Just give us a minute to indulge it. We'll be fine in a sec.'

I chewed my lip. They'd only had all bloody night to indulge it, but whatever. 'Where's Dan?' I asked, for something to say while my parents were having their private what-if grief party.

'He stayed at Oscar's last night. We came up with Ashley's mum.'

The weirdness of my parents and Ashley's mum being in the same car was temporarily eclipsed by my realization that I hadn't even thought about Ash. I whipped round, coughing as I choked on my own anticipation. She was propped up on pillows, eating a bowl of cereal. She looked grey and tired, but otherwise pretty good, considering.

'All right, life-saver,' she said, without looking up from her breakfast. 'Fancy seeing you here.'

I beamed. Never had watching someone drip milk and Rice Krispies on to their chin given me so much pleasure. 'How are you?'

She smiled. 'Oh, all right.' She looked at me and giggled, but then she hiccuped and her eyes filled with tears. I jumped up, took her bowl from her and put it on the bedside table, then got into bed beside her. Covering us both with the sheet, I said, 'You'd better bloody be wearing knickers under that nightie.'

Ash squeezed the tears out of her eyes with the splayed fingers of one hand. 'What, in case I decide to cross lesbo sex off my list?'

'Exactly. I might be a good enough friend to watch you nearly drown yourself, but I draw the line at rudies.'

Ashley curled her hand around mine. Something had changed. The balance between us had shifted. I wasn't yet sure if this was a good thing.

'Anyway,' I said. 'Where's your mum?'

'Gone to the shop. She was doing my head in.'

'Did you know she got a lift with my mum and dad?' I glanced across at them. They were still there, watching me with half-smiles on their faces. Not too weird, then. I gave them a quick smile and turned back to Ashley. She widened her eyes but spoke quietly.

'Yeah. Apparently your parents are a "lovely couple".' She did the speech marks thing, which seemed slightly unnecessary. Like, they *are* a lovely couple. 'I suppose they think my mum's a tanorexic try-hard,' she whispered so they couldn't hear.

'What? No!' I protested, but to be honest they probably did. In the end they just weren't fake-tan-and-false-nails kind of people.

Ashley shrugged. 'They'd be right.'

I shifted in the bed. This wasn't how I'd imagined this conversation going. I suppose I'd secretly expected tearful thanks, heartfelt gratitude from her mum – maybe even a news reporter wanting my story. Moody Ashley was not in the script.

I eyed her as she bit off split ends. I wanted to ask her what it felt like to believe she was going to die, or if she'd had any near-death visions, or if she remembered any of being rescued and having mouth-to-mouth, but I couldn't. It's like if you see someone with no hair and a headscarf, you don't march up and say, 'So what's it like having cancer, then?' I mean, I couldn't be sure it wasn't insensitive to bring it up at all.

So in the end I settled for the boring but safe 'How are you feeling?'

She smiled briefly. 'Shit . . . But, y'know –' she gave me lazy jazz hands – 'alive.'

Later that day the others came to visit. Ashley had spent most of the morning sleeping while I'd dozed and flicked through a few magazines. Mum and Dad had gone to find a hotel and get some sleep, even though the nurses reckoned I'd be discharged that day. I'd felt strangely gutted when they left, but I was kind of too knackered to worry about it.

Anyway, when Cass, Donna, Rich, Ollie and Jack arrived they found me and Ashley sitting up in bed, troughing some surprisingly OK cheesy tomato pasta for lunch. They formed a circle round our beds, which was a bit weird but I suppose that's how it's done, the visiting-invalids thing. Ash had shot me a quick eyebrow-raise when they'd first come in. Like: *Hmm, what'll this be like?* I knew how she felt. And they did all seem kind of nervous at first, taking it in turns to give us both hugs.

Rich teared up a bit, bless him, and even Donna, who held on to Ashley for ages, was a bit moist round the eye area when she pulled away. 'Fuck's sake, you'll do anything for a bit of attention,' she said, quickly brushing away the tears with the back of her hand.

Ash laughed, in a tired kind of way. 'Yeah, I'm thinking of walking down the motorway next time.'

Then Donna threw herself at me. 'And bless YOU, missus.' I hugged her back, blushing but loving it. Who wouldn't?

'Yeah, you're amazing, hon,' said Cass, smiling at me. 'We're so proud of you.'

'And Jack . . .' I prompted, reaching out my hand to take his. 'He's the real life-saver.'

'Don't be silly,' he said quietly. 'You did just as much.'

Rich flung his arm round Jack's shoulders. 'You're a hero, mate. You both are.' I beamed and bit my lip; Jack just smiled and looked at the floor.

'Anyway,' said Cass, putting a box of Celebrations on the bedside table. 'We got you these. I wanted to get you Heroes, but Donna vetoed.'

'Yeah, totally,' said Donna. 'Way too obvious.'

'Any chocolate's fine with me,' I said, tearing open the box and pouring them on to my bed. 'Help yourselves.'

'Um, they're for Ashley too, of course,' said Cass.

I blushed. 'Yeah, course. You don't mind if we share them out, do you?'

Ashley shrugged and nodded, but didn't take one.

Cass chose a mini Mars and perched on the end of Ash's bed. 'So how are you, hon, if that's not a stupid question?'

Ash pulled herself up a bit straighter and smoothed the sheets over her thighs. 'I suppose I'm pretty good, considering the nearly dying stuff . . . I can't seem to get enough sleep, but apart from that . . . Yeah, I feel all right.'

Cass's eyes darted to the others, and Donna and Rich kind of nodded encouragingly. 'Are you OK to tell us what happened?' she added gently. Ah, now I understood. They must have had a discussion about whether or not it was all right to ask. I didn't blame them. After all, I couldn't bring myself to ask and I was there.

'Not much to tell, to be honest,' said Ashley. 'I got cramp. I'd never had it before, so I kind of freaked. It was like something was attacking me.' She shook her head at the memory. 'I thought I was . . . done for.' She widened her eyes and waggled her fingers ironically, but her eyes did look scared. Poor her, she really had been through something terrifying. I couldn't imagine what it must feel like to actually believe that your time was up.

'Thank God for you, babes,' said Cass, reaching over and patting my leg.

I shrugged. 'Right place at the right time. I didn't even think about it – I just went in.' I told them the whole story. It felt good to voice it all. I swear I didn't embellish it, but I saw Donna gave Rich a look, like I was loving it. I didn't really care. She was probably just jealous. She loved being the centre of attention.

I looked over at Ollie, who hadn't said a word. 'You all right, Ols?'

He blinked and cleared his throat. 'Yeah, fine. Just glad you're all right.' He attempted a watery smile. Aw, what a softy. Who'd have thought Ollie would get emotional?

'What about you, Jack?' I said. 'How come you turned up in the nick of time? I've been going over and over it in my head and I just can't work it out.'

He hunched his shoulders, his hands stuffed into his jeans pockets. 'I was looking for my scarf – I left it when we were playing volleyball. Then I recognized your bag and Ashley's coat . . .' He tailed off.

'Oh, riiiight,' I said. 'God, I'd been thinking you were, like, psychic or something. But, shit, thank God you left your scarf . . . I might have got Ashley out of the water, but I'd have been useless at the mouth-to-mouth stuff.' It was probably part of the life-saving badge all those years ago, but I couldn't remember any of it.

Jack shrugged. 'We both did what we had to do.' He seemed genuinely uncomfortable, like he'd rather we didn't go on about it. Honestly, I could have talked about it all day. Maybe it was cos Jack was so into sport that it wasn't all that to him – physical exertion was what he was all about, and he put on his life-saver guise every time he went to work at the swimming pool – but this might be the one amazing thing I do in my whole life. I was more than happy to milk it.

As we paused in a moment of awkward silence, a nurse appeared to tell me and Ash that the consultant was on her way to see us. Cue friends' departure.

'We'll come and see you tomorrow,' said Cass. 'Look after yourselves.'

'Can't really do anything else in this place,' said Ashley. 'But thanks. You too.'

Another quick round of hugs, and they disappeared, leaving the ward feeling very quiet and empty. I wondered where they were going now. The hostel and the beach seemed to belong in some kind of parallel universe since I'd been in here.

I started to say as much to Ashley, but she had her eyes closed again. It worried me to see her like this. Obviously she'd be in intensive care if the doctors thought there was a problem, but still. What if the water had done some kind of terrible damage to her lungs and no one had noticed? As I waited for the consultant I watched Ashley's chest rise and fall, and tried not to think about what could have been – or what might be.

12

Hi Joe. On way home from
Devon early. Have been in
hospital – long story. All
OK tho. Can't wait 2 see u
xxx

Shit what happened? Jx

Ash got into trouble in
the sea n I got her out. I
had mild hypothermia but
fine now xxx

No end to your talents
babes ;) Glad you're ok x

Me too! C u thurs.
Looking fwd to some tlc
dot dot dot! Xxx : p

Facebook status update
Sarah Millar: is thinking winter swimming ain't all that.

Comments:
Cass Henderson: LOL me too! V glad you're OK, hero lady! Xx

Hey Sarah. You home yet?
Devon not same without
u! Xxx

Aw fanks Cass. In car with
Ash n her mum. Ash
asleep. Bless her think
she's still knackered x

Bet she is. She was v
quiet in hospital but
guess that's not surpris-
ing. She's lucky 2 have u
n Jack x

Hmm not sure she thinks
that! xx

What do u mean? What's
she said? x

Nothing! Hasn't even said
thanks. Don't expect lots
but something would be
nice! x

Weird. Don't worry bout it
hun. She's prob in shock.
Give her time xx

I know. You're right. So
what u lot up to? xx

Donna n Rich gone back
to bed wiv hangover,
Ollie, me n Jack in cafe
eating cream tea! xx

Oh NO jealous! Can't
believe i'm missing
scones! You back day
after tomorrow? x

Yep. Will call u then. Look
after yourself hun. Have
fun with Joe!!! xxxx

I so will! Can't WAIT 2 see
him. Enjoy rest of hol
sobs xxx

LOL xx

———

Oi McSarey how r u
feeling? How r plans for
world domination coming
on??

Haha v funny Ols. Altho
am considering pants-
over-leggings superhero
combo. V fetching no?

No.

Haha. *Slaps Ollie upside
the head*

Cries like girl

Yeah well. Let that be
lesson 2 u. Hope you're
able to enjoy Devon despite
me-shaped hole in it.

R u kidding? It's a freakin
riot. Even as we speak am
eating scones SCONES I
TELL U.

All right no need to rub it
in. Am going to sleep
now but not at all cos
you're boring me. No
way. *snores*

Aw shit, my sides have
split. Later dude x

Later x

———

Hey Jack, how r u? Do u
still feel weird?? I really
do. Seems unreal x

Hi Sarah i know really
weird n unreal. Am
trying not 2 think about
it! It's strange here
without u n Ash. She
OK? x

GIRL HEART BOY

Yeah she's fine. Sleeping
in car at mo. Look after
yourself. C u at school x

Yes c u then. Have fun at
Joe's x

13

Within twenty-four hours we were back in Brighton, and Devon was miles away in every sense. It felt like it had happened to other people.

The journey back had been quiet. I spent the journey texting and thinking about Joe. Imagining what it'd be like to see him again. Just two more days. I couldn't wait. Like, literally couldn't wait. The following forty-eight hours were full of sinister potential. What if I was run over by a bus before I got to see him again? My whole life was focussed on the moment I got on the train to London.

Back in Brighton we dropped Ashley and her mum at theirs, picked up Daniel from his friend's, then went home, where the house was quiet and cold and Dan stared at me like I was an alien. Mum cooked cheese on toast and made me eat it on a tray in bed like an invalid. I felt fine, although tired. I finished my toast then fell asleep again.

I woke up nine hours later to torrential rain and a too-much-sleep headache. I couldn't stop thinking about the hospital. I felt almost nostalgic for it, with its routine and regular meals and me and Ash in our own little bubble. I tried not to think about the event that got us there, although 'I saved someone's life' kept appearing in my mind like someone walking across the front of a stage with a placard. It made my stomach pitch in fear and disbelief and, if I'm honest, excitement and pride.

My bedroom was closing in on me. The doctor at the hospital had told Mum and Dad that I needed to take it easy, which they saw as a free pass to keep me bedridden. Everything in my room was annoying. My purple duvet cover, the books on the shelves with the S-shaped book-ends, the photo collages of me and my friends . . . Childish and routine. Even the smell of my pillow was claustrophobically familiar. I missed the strangeness of the hospital. Missed feeling special. I stared at the ceiling, lethargy draped over me like a concrete blanket. My phone was on my chest, where I'd dropped it when there wasn't a single thing left I could bear to watch on iPlayer. It wasn't even as if I could have nice long conversations with Joe – maybe even pick up where we left off, phone-sex wise – since Joe was in one of his rubbish phases on the contact front. I supposed there was no need for him to get in touch: I was seeing him tomorrow.

Tomorrow! Flicking to Favourites, I clicked on his

name, and then instantly ended the call when my mum barged in. Well, not barged exactly. She's not a barging kind of person. But, like, there's no point knocking if you don't wait for a response. She put a pile of clothes on my desk. 'Here's your Devon stuff, all washed.'

Whoop-di-doo. 'Thanks.'

She stood for a moment, hand on hip, watching me. I stared back. She folded her arms. 'How are you feeling?'

'Oh, you know.' I sighed, smiling tightly. 'Still completely fine and still going mental stuck in here.'

Mum sat on the edge of my bed and stroked my hair. I tried not to flinch. 'You've had a traumatic experience,' she said. 'Your body needs time to recover.'

'Uh-huh.' I'd heard it approximately two hundred and forty-eight times before.

'Just a couple more days taking it easy, darling. You can watch the telly in our room if you want.' She started opening drawers and putting my clothes away.

'Thanks, but there's only so much *Cash in the Attic* I can take . . .' She carefully placed a symmetrically folded pile of knickers in my drawer. 'Mum, don't. I'll do it . . .' Although I wouldn't have. Just watching her made me feel tired. 'Anyway, I'm nearly eighteen years old,' I complained, returning to the incarceration issue. 'I think I can just about tell if I'm ill or not.'

She'd moved on to tidying my desk now. It was hair-tearingly irritating. She paused in the middle of dusting my lamp with a spat-on tissue. 'Obviously we can't keep you here, Sarah, but you're not an adult yet. Whether you like it or not, we probably still know what's best for you –' She put her hand up and talked over my spluttering indignation. 'As far as your health is concerned, anyway.'

I sagged back on my bed. I was too bloody obedient for my own good. Then I very speedily unsagged, sitting up so fast I got a head rush. 'I can't stay in bed for two more days! I'm going to London tomorrow.'

Mum didn't pause from her tidying frenzy. 'Not this time, you're not. The girls will understand.'

I started to cry. I couldn't help it. Mum looked at me, surprised, then came and sat on the edge of my bed. 'Sweetheart, you've had a dreadful shock. You're bound to be emotional.' She put her hand on my forehead and I put out my arms so she could hug me. I wanted her to tell me it'd all be OK.

'It's not the shock,' I hiccuped into her shoulder.

'What is it then?' asked Mum, gently.

I paused, smelling her familiar Mum smell and imagining the concern on her face. It was no good, I couldn't tell her about Joe. The thought of all the questions then, when they'd got used to the idea, the *we're so liberal* enthusiasm and jovial teasing . . . I'd have cringed myself to death.

'I just want to get back to normal . . . be with my friends. It's been arranged for weeks.' I made a huge effort to keep my voice calm – getting hysterical would not help my case – but the thought of not being able to see Joe! I was this far from whimpering with panic.

Mum disengaged from our hug and put on her practical face. 'There's no need to get so het up. Just re-arrange for the weekend.'

'I can't,' I growled. 'Donna's with her mum and Cass is seeing Adam.'

'Well, I'm sorry, darling. They'll have to go without you, just this once.'

I took a breath and smoothed the material of my PJ bottoms. Keeping my voice low, I said, 'Look, I'm fine. The hospital wouldn't have let me come all the way back home if they didn't think I was OK. We're not planning on doing anything strenuous. We're just going to do a bit of shopping, stay at Donna's cous-in's place, then come home.'

'You're staying over!' Mum said, her voice going squeaky.

'Yes, I told you that,' I said through gritted teeth.

She walked to the door, gearing up for the last

word. 'I'm sorry, Sarah, but you're not going. Trust us, this is the right thing to do. It's either miss one occasion with your friends, or miss lots because you didn't take the time to recover properly.' And out she went, closing the door with a gentle click to show how calm and in control and right she was.

I burst into tears again. I had to see Joe. Had to. I couldn't believe this half term, with all its potential, was turning out to be so crap.

After five minutes of messy sobbing, I blew my nose and lay in exhausted moodiness, considering my options. And then almost immediately thought, sod it, and phoned Joe. I was gearing up to leave a message when, incredibly, he answered.

'Sarah.' His voice saying my name was just about the sexiest thing I'd ever heard.

'Joe. How's it going?' I realized I was involuntarily licking my phone, which was not only deeply weird but probably also deeply unhygienic. I stopped, if only because I didn't want Joe wondering what the strange slurping noise was.

'Yeah, good thanks, babes. We still on for Thursday?' He lowered his voice. 'I plan to keep you naked for forty-eight hours straight.'

I closed my eyes with lust and disappointment. Possibly the least satisfying combo in the history of

the world ever. 'I'm so sorry, Joe, I can't come . . . The
doctor says I have to stay in bed until Friday.' There
was silence on the end of the line. I chewed my lip.

'I'm on my way.'

I swallowed. 'Sorry?'

'I said I'll come to you.' I could hear the smile in
his voice. 'No probs, babes.'

Nought to sixty in ten seconds. I wanted to dance
in a shaft of sunlight, my shiny hair bouncing fra-
grantly. 'Oh yeah, wow, that'd be brilliant!' I enthused,
all my friends' advice about playing it cool forgotten.

'Great. I'll text from the train . . . Just one thing –
exactly how sick are you, Sarah Doesn't-like-beer?'

I smiled. 'Don't worry. A bit of exercise is probably just what I need . . . I'll still be in bed, right?'

'And on the floor, across the desk, against the
wall . . .'

After I'd ended the call and lain for a while in a swoon
of unbridled lust, the reality of my little Romeo and
Juliet scenario reared its annoying head. Namely,
what was I going to tell my parents? How to explain
that Joe was paying a visit? Yes, the Joe from Spain –
did I not tell you we were together? Oops, must have
slipped my mind. Oh and, by the way, we'll be alone
in my locked bedroom. No matter what I came up
with, it never ended well. As I was pondering if there

was any way I could persuade Mum and Dad to take Daniel out for the night, Mum poked her head round the door.

'We won't be late, darling. There's some spag bol for you and Dan on the side. You just need to give it a couple of minutes in the microwave.'

I sat up. 'Wait, where are you going?'

Mum came into the room properly. She was wearing her beaded cardigan and lipgloss. 'To the theatre with Steph and Mark. I told you last night . . .' Her forehead creased. 'We can cancel if you want.'

'No! No no no,' I said hurriedly. 'I remember now. Have fun!' I smiled brightly.

Mum hesitated. 'You're sure?'

I nodded manically like the Churchill dog. She paused for a moment and my heart paused with her, but then she gave a little wave and disappeared. Now that is what I call a result! I waited till I heard the front door click shut then ran downstairs to find Dan. It felt good to be using my legs again. He was on his Xbox in the living room, where he always was if wasn't doing dodgy Google searches.

'All right, Dan?' I asked. He ignored me. I suppressed the urge to give him a slap and scowled at the greasy, dandruff-flecked back of his head. Someone needed to give the kid a lesson in personal hygiene. Puberty was definitely rearing its ugly head. Ugh, the thought made me want to vom. Deciding to wait this one out, I went and sat next to him on the sofa. After a couple of minutes there was a massive explosion on the screen, limbs flying everywhere. Game Over. He turned to me.

'What?'

I smiled. 'Nothing. Just bored upstairs on my own.'

He grunted. 'Mum and Dad say I've got to give you time to get over your trauma.'

'Do they now?' I pulled my legs up under me.

The seconds ticked away. 'Was it scary . . . being in the sea?' he asked, suddenly looking like a little kid again.

'Not at the time. It was afterwards, though.'

He looked down at the control in his hands. 'Well . . . I'm glad you're OK.'

I smiled, surprised. Shocked, even. 'Thanks, Dan. I'm glad I'm OK too . . .' I shifted so I was facing him. 'Actually, I've got a favour to ask.'

He looked bemused. 'What?'

'Promise you won't tell Mum and Dad?' That did it. I had his full attention now.

'Promise.'

'Dan, this is really important. I have to be able to trust you on this.' I gave him some serious eye contact, and he frowned irritably.

'I *said* I promise.'

'Good. OK. Well, the thing is . . .' How to put this?

'The thing is I've got someone coming to see me here, tonight. And I really need you to stay downstairs while he's here.' I looked at the control in his hand. 'I'll get you a new Xbox game if you do.'

'"He"? Is it your boyfriend? You want me to stay down here so you can shag him in your bedroom, don't you?'

I paused. 'Yes.'

He switched his game on again. 'Yeah, no worries.'

Huh. That had been easier than I expected.

'But if you want me to keep quiet, I want two new games.' His eyes were fixed on the screen.

'We agreed on one new game.' You little shit.

He shrugged. 'Take it or leave it.'

I sighed. 'Fine. But if you even show your face when Joe's here I'll tell Mum and Dad you've been smoking.'

'All right, all right, I said I'd stay out of your way, didn't I?' He made a retching face. 'Anyway I don't want to see him. He must be ugly or mental – or both – to want to shag you.'

'Whatever. Dickhead.'

'Bitch.'

'Anyway. He'll be here soon so . . .'

'Stay in here. I know.' He made a face but I ignored it. Mission accomplished! Let Operation Romeo and Juliet commence.

But I was jogging upstairs to run a bath, thinking how Joe must be just about on the train by now, when he called.

'Hey, sexy,' I purred. (Well, he'd started it. All that stuff about nakedness and desks.)

'Babes, I'm really sorry, I can't come after all.' He sounded gutted. But not as gutted as me.

'Why not?' I didn't even bother keeping the disappointment out of my voice.

'Work's just phoned – someone's off sick and they need me to cover . . . I can't afford to turn it down.'

It seemed almost inevitable. Of course we weren't going to see each other. It never worked out for us. And now I was left facing an evening in with my irritating little brother, Mr Nosepicker himself. Could things get any worse?

14

I trudged back downstairs to tell Dan the good news.

'We'll just make it one Xbox game, then,' he said, still not taking his eyes off the screen.

'What? No way! I'm not buying you any bloody games.' I almost laughed. The cheek!

He shrugged. 'I'll tell Mum and Dad you had a boy coming here tonight, then.'

I narrowed my eyes. 'They wouldn't believe you.'

'Why would I lie?'

When did my baby brother turn into such a cunning little bastard? I slumped down on the sofa beside him. This was turning out to be the worst day ever. 'Tell them what you like, I'm past caring,' I said, sighing.

'So who is this Joe, anyway?' asked Dan, pausing the action.

I exhaled moodily. 'I met him in Spain.'

Dan grimaced. 'What, that skinny posh guy?' I nodded. 'You're shagging him?' He laughed. 'It must be like Baloo shagging Mowgli.'

I curled my lip in disgust. 'Firstly, that's sick. Secondly, stop saying "shag". And thirdly, I'm not fat . . .'

'Not much.'

I ignored him. One of his squibby little friends had obviously told him that the way to wind a big sister up was to tell her she's fat. Well, it wouldn't work on me. God, I had insecurities enough. He'd just have to do his research. I wiped my hand across my eyes. I couldn't believe I wasn't going to see Joe AGAIN.

'Aw, missing Joey-woey?' crooned Dan.

I gave him a slap. 'Shut up, dick.'

'OW! I'm telling Mum.' He rubbed his head.

'Say what you like,' I said again. Misery misery. I sighed deeply. 'You'll understand one day, in the unlikely event of you turning into an attractive human being.'

'I've kissed three girls, actually,' he sniffed. 'With tongues. And one of them let me touch her tit.'

How disgusting. 'Well, I hope she washed it afterwards,' I said wearily. This was not making me feel better, but anything was preferable to moping in my room. I was sick of the sight of it. I sat in miserable silence while the mindless music, gun noises and explosions of Dan's game filled the room. Then my phone rang again. Joe.

I got up and left the room, Dan so engrossed in gunning down Germans that I don't think he even noticed. I answered the phone. 'Hey.'

'Babe, I've just had a thought. Why don't you come up here this weekend instead? I'm working Saturday night, but you can amuse yourself for a few hours, right?'

'Right, yeah, of course,' I said quickly, the emotional rollercoaster that was my life on a sudden upwards slant. 'That works out better for me, actually. I'll get the train Saturday morning, like last time.'

'That's great, babe. Brilliant. See you then, yeah?'

'Yeah. I'll text from the train.' But he'd hung up.

I mused indulgently for a moment on the rubbishness of boys on the phone, but my thoughts quickly turned to the weekend. Having two days to prepare meant I could shave my legs and take time deciding what to wear – maybe even order some new underwear online. No, it was definitely a good thing that Joe couldn't come today. Hadn't Mum herself suggested that I go up to London this weekend? I beamed at the cheesy photo of me in dungarees, aged five, which had been on the wall at the bottom of the stairs for as long as I could remember. It was about time my luck changed.

Seeing Joe again was just as amazing as I'd imagined it. It was like we'd never been apart. He didn't meet me at the station this time. I'd told him not to. I didn't want him thinking I was some provincial girl who was scared of London. (Not that he came from the ghetto. He was from somewhere in Surrey I'd never heard of, but come on: Surrey? Not exactly urban jungle.) I got the Tube up to his house no probs, and within approximately ninety-four seconds of arriving at his place we were rolling naked on the floor of his room. It was brilliant: sweaty, ravenous, breathy-moany sex. I felt utterly, completely free. It was like I was released from myself. I wasn't Sarah: virginal, feminist, gullible but nice. I was feelings and sounds and skin-on-skin. I didn't care that my face was red and scrunched, because Joe's was too. Everything was the two of us. My friends, my parents, my brother . . . they were a part of my life I could think about indulgently – it was nice to have them. But they were a lucky extra. It was all about us: me and Joe.

All this went through my head as we lay afterwards on Joe's floor, his duvet pulled on top of us. He tickled my forehead with the tip of his finger. 'What are you thinking?'

Not my favourite question. I never want to give an honest answer, because I'm usually thinking something stupid like, *Would my legs look like skittles in harem pants? Or, What if my dreams are real and real life is actually the dream?*

I sighed contentedly and snuggled into him.

'Nothing, really . . . Just how nice this is.' Which was at least a condensed version of the truth.

He kissed my head. 'You're sweet.' I closed my eyes. It was going to be OK between us. How could it not?

When I woke up it was dark outside and I was stiff from lying on the floor. I dragged myself and the duvet back on to the bed. It felt like the warmest, cosiest place in the world. The toilet flushed and Joe came back in, dressed and with hair wet from the shower. He sat on the edge of the bed and took my hand. Seeing the expression on his face sent my insides plummeting.

'I'm so sorry, babes, but work's asked me to do all day tomorrow as well as tonight.' He squeezed my fingers. 'You know I can't turn it down.'

I smiled bravely. I would not be clingy. 'That's OK. I'll just wait for you to come back tonight then leave when you go to work in the morning.'

He ran his hand down my throat and across the top of my chest. 'Honestly, it'd be better if you went today. I won't be back till gone midnight and I'll just want to sleep.' He moved his hand under the duvet to squeeze my breast and lowered his voice. 'You're a bad influence.'

I knew when I was being patronized, but I wasn't

angry. Just sad. The memory of Mimi's expression at the party hovered like a sign warning me to play it cool. Maybe this was how some relationships worked. Cass and Adam's wasn't like this, but who'd want to be like them?

I slid my hand under the waist of Joe's jeans and kissed his shoulder. 'Maybe we should have one more go before you leave?'

He plucked my arm away by the wrist and stood up, almost irritably. 'C'mon, babe, I've got to go.' He kissed the side of my head. 'I'll call you soon, yeah? Take your time leaving. There's bread for toast, I think.'

'Right. Bye then,' I said, bleakly, to his retreating back. I hadn't even had a chance to confront him about telling Mimi our secrets, which I really had meant to do. I stared into space until I heard the front door click shut and then, naked on my own in an empty house in this city of a gazillion people, I cried. I got out of bed, pulled on my clothes without showering and left the house. I just wanted to be away from there, and away from London. I was still snivelling as I walked from Joe's house to the station. Keeping an eye out for potential phone-snatchers, I scrolled through my Favourites. Ashley, Cass, Donna . . . I didn't want to speak to any of them. Jack? He'd just be freaked out. Rich was a no-no – he already had enough on his mind. My thumb hovered over Ollie's name. He was funny and he didn't judge. I connected the call and he answered almost straight away.

'Hairy McSarey, shouldn't you be doing unspeakable things with Joe?'

I tried to laugh, but it came out kind of phlegmy.

'Wait . . . you OK, flower?'

Oh lovely, lovely Ollie. Why couldn't we fancy each other instead? I cleared my throat and forced myself to sound bright, although I think it veered more towards highly strung and mental. 'Yeah, fine. Just walking to the station from Joe's actually.' There was a pause. Why had I phoned? I'd never called him for a chat before. That's not what you did with boys. I swallowed. 'Anyway. Uh . . . just wondered what you were doing tomorrow?' I heard crackling noises down the phone followed by wet crunching. Ollie eating crisps in surround sound. Nice.

'Not much,' he said around a mouthful of (probably) Ready Salted. 'Sleeping late. Watching telly . . . Why?'

Good question. 'Well . . . uh . . . I was thinking of getting us all together for a kind of post-Devon thing. Before we go back to school. Type thing.' Nice one, Sarah. Eloquent.

'Yeah, count me in. Are the others coming?'

'Dunno. You're the first one I phoned, actually.' I let my head drop back and shook it despairingly at the heavy late-autumn clouds.

'Aw, McSarey, I didn't know you cared.'

I sniffed. 'Yeah, you're all right. Listen, I'll text you when I know what's happening, 'K?' I'd reached the station. The display told me that another train was going in two minutes. Suddenly being on that train was the most important thing ever. I jigged up and down on the spot, as if that would hurry Ollie up.

'Cool,' he said. 'You sure you're OK, flower?'

My eyes welled up. Damn him for being so nice. 'Yeah, no, fine. Totally. I'll see you tomorrow.' I tucked my phone into its special pocket in my rucksack, wiped my eyes with my sleeve and legged it down the stairs to the platform. I leapt on to the train just as the doors were closing, found an empty seat and slumped into it. Joe would be at work by now, smiling at strangers, chatting with his workmates behind the bar. I wished I was with him so much it hurt.

15

Sitting on the sofas in Costa the next day with my friends, I wished I'd never suggested meeting up. Never had a day seemed more Sundayish. It was freezing cold and the sky was heavy and grey, my eyes felt tired from crying myself to sleep the night before, and everything that ever annoyed me about my friends was annoying me now. Cass was going on about Adam – he's so different recently, he's really settling down, he really loves me. Meh meh. Right. Until the next time he shags a slapper in a nightclub. Ash had taken her boots and socks off and was sitting cross-legged and barefoot on the sofa. We were in a high-street coffee shop – there was really no need to be so bloody alternative the WHOLE FREAKING TIME. Donna was nursing a hangover and banging on about her great night and how she'd been like reeeeally hammered. YAWN. Rich was depressed and grouchy – a hangover too, but not from booze. Jack was sickeningly upbeat after winning some football match that morning, and Ollie was obliviously eating the foam off his cappuccino with a spoon.

I slouched in the corner of the sofa and checked Mimi's Facebook. She didn't have any privacy settings, leaving me free to snoop around at will. There was nothing much new on there. A couple of wall exchanges. Her status said: 'Mimi Sedgwick is the most . . . to say the least'. Eight people Liked it and it had six comments, one of which said, 'Meemsy meemsy moo i love yoooooooooooou.' I turned my phone off in disgust, then immediately turned it on again in case Joe texted. I fired off another to him for good measure – the third since I'd left him yesterday, but I was past caring.

> OMG today is booooooring.
> Hope yours is better xx

I deleted all the extra 'o's in boring, then added them in again. He still hadn't accepted my Facebook friend request, but that's probably because he never went on it. He hadn't changed his profile pic since I'd known him (a picture of Stewie, the evil baby from *Family Guy*).

'Uh, SARAH?'

I looked up, surprised. I was engrossed in Googling Joe's family. Both his parents were lawyers. I thought lawyers earned a fortune, but maybe they were the type who thought their children should fend for themselves to learn the true value of money blah

blah. I clicked my screen off and blinked at the faces all looking at me expectantly.

'Yeah?'

'Ollie was just saying he's having a bonfire-night party at his house?' Ashley stared at me with heavy eyelids. Her not-impressed face.

'Oh. Right. Good idea,' I said, and met her gaze. Her eyes didn't falter, and I looked away first, my face flushing. What just happened? Were we arguing?

'Uh, yeah,' said Ollie, his eyes flickering from Ash's face to mine. 'The house'll be empty, so . . .' He spread his hands and smiled.

'Can Joe come?' Having an actual event to invite Joe to could be just what I needed to pin him down. I swear Ashley, Donna and Cass exchanged a rolly-eyes look, but they could piss off. They were just . . . Well, actually I didn't know what their problem was. But still. They could piss off anyway.

Ollie shrugged. 'More the merrier.'

I beamed at him. 'Thanks, Ol.' As the others started talking among themselves again, I turned back to my phone and texted Joe.

> Btw bonfire night house
> party here Sat 5th Nov.
> Presume i should add u
> to guestlist??xxx

When I looked up, Cass and Donna were shrugging on their coats and Ashley was buckling her boots. 'You off?' I asked, suddenly not wanting them to go. At least, not like this, without me.

'Yeah, thought we might catch a matinee at the cinema,' said Donna, looking down as she zipped up her jacket.

'Oh . . . OK.' I don't know why I couldn't just say I'd join them. Normally I would have, but something about the way they wouldn't catch my eye made me feel like it wasn't an option. Cass asked me if I wanted to come, but I'm sure Ashley shot her a look. First Joe, now my friends. It was getting very tiring trying to be low-maintenance about everything.

After they left I blinked rapidly, drank a few gulps of tea and cleared my throat while scratching my eyebrow. *Et voilà*: the tears disappeared. I stood up. 'So. I should be off too. I've got a French translation.' I stretched my mouth into some semblance of a smile and, without looking at any of the boys, weaved through the tables and out the door.

'All right, babes?' It was the first day back at school after half term and Ashley had just sat down beside me at our usual table in the maths room and cracked open a can of Diet Coke. 'Feels like ages since we last sat here.'

It did. I couldn't believe our daring sea rescue had

happened less than a week ago. I smiled at her, happy that things were back to normal. Everyone was allowed to be moody every now and then. Didn't mean you hated them forever.

Ash offered me her drink. I shook my head. 'How was the film?'

'Shit. You didn't miss anything.'

I wondered whether it was OK to talk about Devon and decided to risk it. I was feeling brave after getting through yesterday's weirdness. 'So are you, like, totally better now?'

She rocked back on her chair and braced one foot against the table. There was a sticker stuck to the sole of her boot. It had a picture of a grinning cartoon crocodile with 'I look after my teeth' written above it. 'Yeah, no, totally. I've got to go back to the doc's tomorrow for a check, but . . . yeah, I'm fine.' She paused. 'Look, I haven't even thanked you yet for . . . what you did. You know I'm really grateful, right?' She smiled at me, almost shyly. It was good to hear, but before I could answer she looked in the direction of the door and said, 'Whoa. Somebody's keen.'

Not only was our tutor alarmingly early but he also made a beeline for our desk, pulling out a chair and sitting astride it backwards, his legs either side of the backrest. I smirked and caught Ashley's eye. Really, the man was a tit.

'So, dramatic half term then, yah?' he said to Ash.

'Yah, I suppose you could say that.'

'Well, you just take it easy this week, hmm? No physical exertions.' He smirked, possibly sleazily.

Ash raised an eyebrow. 'Right. Thanks, Paul.'

'All your teachers are aware of your . . . situation, so not to worry if you need to sit a lesson out, just for the next week or so while you're getting back on your feet.' And with that he did a monumentally cheesy wink and double tongue click and left the room. It was only five minutes till he needed to take the register, but whatever. Busy busy busy.

Ash watched him leave. 'Does he think I've had a backstreet abortion?' she said, shaking her head. She adopted Paul's lopsided smirk. 'Your "situation"? Shit.'

'He's an idiot,' I agreed.

'I really don't want to make a big thing out of this,' said Ash seriously. 'Honestly, I just want to forget it ever happened. Move on, you know?'

'Yeah, course,' I said, although a part of me (the same shameful part that hoped for a media circus at the hospital) felt strangely hurt.

I went to the field by myself at lunchtime. I wanted to be able to call Joe and check my phone in peace. He didn't answer – obvs – so I texted:

> Ollie wants to finalize
> numbers for 5 nov party.
> You coming? There will be
> fit girls (i.e. me)

I had another look at Mimi's Facebook while I ate my sandwich. Her status was something boring about her phone being out of action. I was about to look up Joe's uni website when I got a reply:

> Sounds good. Shd be fine
> but need to check x

I did a bit of a squeal and, chucking the remains of my sandwich into the bushes that lined the school field, ran back to the canteen.

'Where've you been?' asked Cass, pulling her bag off the chair they'd saved me.

'Just had to do a bit of research . . . Where's Ollie?'

'Loo.'

'Oh good, I wanted to tell him that Joe's coming to his party.' I peeled back the lid of the yogurt I'd just bought and sniffed it. 'Does this smell funny?' I held it out to the table at large.

Donna snatched it off me and stuck her nose into the pot. 'It's fine.' She handed it back, but I pushed it to one side. Milk and yogurt have to be in tip-top condition if they're going to pass my lips. Otherwise you might as well be drinking rancid phlegm.

'Yeah, Joe's really up for it,' I continued. 'You'll really like him. He's really sweet and, like, witty, y'know? Right, Ash? God, I can't believe you're the only one who's met him!'

Ashley shrugged. 'Yeah well, I haven't actually met him properly.'

I sat up straight in my seat. 'Oh my God, it was sooo funny. We were on our way to his house on Saturday, on the Tube, and he kept pretending to scratch his cheek but actually giving me the finger, you know? I was pissing myself. The other people on the train must've thought I was mental.' I chuckled, but nobody joined in. Cass, Jack and Rich were kind of smiling encouragingly, like they were waiting for a punchline, but Ash and Donna were expressionless.

'Guess you had to be there, Sar,' said Ash. She nodded at my manky yogurt. 'You going to eat that?' I pushed it towards her. I cleared my throat and fluffed the back of my hair casually. She was right – it was a crap story. And a total lie. I just wanted an anecdote to offer them that didn't involve sex or, y'know, disappointment. Me and Joe just didn't see each other enough, but that would change in time. I stood up.

'Anyway . . . I'm going to get a Twix. Anyone want anything?'

I tried to do cleansing breathing while I was waiting to pay. I hated this. It was like everything I said and did was being stored up by the others to add to some invisible list of crimes I was committing without even knowing it. I tapped my fingers against my teeth. Getting Cass on her own would help. She understood what it was like to have a boyfriend. I'd ask her to come shopping with me after school, I decided. I was skint after Devon, but she always ended up buying something (her parents gave her, like, a £100-a-month clothing allowance), and I could talk about stuff while she was distracted.

Feeling slightly better, I went back to the table. Ollie was there and everyone was discussing if there was a way to have a bonfire in his garden without his parents finding out. This I could help with. My granny and grandpa had bonfires on their allotment all the time.

'You just dig up the grass in, like, flat squares, then put it back when you've finished,' I said through a mouthful of Twix. 'It's not difficult.'

Ollie leant across the table, took my face in his hands and gave me a smacker on the forehead. 'That's what I'm talking about, people. Bit of common sense.' He smiled at me. 'Cheers, flower.'

Next lesson was art history and Andrea, our teacher, sat on the edge of a table, her legs crossed at the knee. She was telling us about Andy Warhol's Factory studio in 1960s New York, where artists, writers and rock stars came to make art and, ahem, 'practise free love'. It was fascinating. Honestly, she totally had the room. Andrea was a good teacher and everyone liked her, and you could tell she was really into the Sixties art scene stuff. She even looked right, with her graphic print headscarf, cargo pants and ballet pumps.

Anyway, one of the photos she showed us was of a woman, not that much older than us, who was Warhol's muse: she inspired him. In the picture this woman's leaning back but sort of thrusting her body upwards. It doesn't look sexual though, cos she's got no boobs to speak of. She's holding a cigarette and a glass of, what, vodka? I guessed it wasn't water, anyway. She's wearing a tight black top and huge black earrings, and staring at the camera with these big, black, Sixties eyes. She looks beautiful and confident and don't-give-a-shit, and everything about her made me feel dull and conventional. Even when we learned that she'd died of a drug overdose when she was twenty-eight, I envied her. I didn't want to take drugs or die young (like, duh) but I wished I could be a bit less . . . obvious. A bit less het up about bloody Joe and my does-he-like-me woes. I sighed wistfully. I would so, so love someone to want me to be their muse. But as Joe, not even an artist but a boring old politics student, seemed to forget me from one day to the next, what hope did I have?

I nibbled at a hangnail. Self-pity is a very ugly emotion, I sternly reminded myself. And Joe hasn't forgotten you, because he's coming to Ollie's bonfire-night party. So get a grip.

After the lesson had finished I hovered outside the door and waited for everyone to leave so I could call Joe. I left a voicemail saying I was looking forward to the party, and could he call or text to make arrangements, and was about to go to the canteen for a mid-afternoon muffin when Andrea came out of the classroom. She was carrying a huge blue-and-white-striped canvas hold-all. In a shop I wouldn't have looked at it twice, but on her shoulder, with her outfit, I wanted it.

'OK, Sarah?' she asked, smiling at me.

'Yes, thanks . . . Uh, I wasn't waiting for you,' I said, and then instantly worried that she hadn't been thinking I was anyway.

'Right, well. Have a good evening!' she said and, feeling strangely disappointed, I watched her walk away from me down the corridor towards the staff room.

'. . . So then I left another message, but he still hasn't got back to me.'

Cass picked up a grey top with tiny silver birds sewn round the hem. She held it up against herself and raised her eyebrows.

I glanced at her. 'Yeah. Really nice,' I said then went back to chewing my cuticles. It was gone five. We'd been shopping for nearly two hours and I was hungry. I hadn't asked Cass why she, Ashley and Donna were being off with me. Now I was here I realized it would have to involve sort of implicating Cass. And not only would that pretty much amount to picking a fight but it'd also be like reinforcing Cass's place with Ash and Donna as the three of them against the one of me. So I was trying to get Cass to sympathize about Joe instead. I thought if I made him out to be a bit crap, she'd want to give me the benefit of her (considerable) experience. After all, we were still the only ones in our group with a boyfriend (or whatever).

Cass folded the top to almost its original perfection and carefully put it back in the pile. She flicked through a pile of different tops. 'Look, Sarah, if you don't want to be here, go home.'

I rubbed my forehead. 'I'm sorry, Cass. I'm just really tired. I haven't been able to sleep much these past couple of days.'

'Yeah, you have mentioned it,' said Cass, almost under her breath. Then: 'What about this one?' She held up the same top in a different colour.

I tried to do nodding with enthusiasm and sat down on the floor. She was obviously going to be a while. I fiddled with my bag strap. 'So . . . I wonder if Joe will call me tonight.'

Cass closed her eyes long-sufferingly. 'I don't know, Sarah. It's impossible to say. His record isn't great, so . . .'

I felt a spark of annoyance. Friends were supposed to be happy to listen to each other's troubles. I'd listened to her bang on about Adam often enough.

'Actually, I think I will make a move.' I leant on the wall as leverage and stood up. 'I've just remembered Mum said she was making tea for half five cos Dan's got Scouts.'

She barely even looked at me. 'Fine. See you tomorrow.'

I tried to catch her eye, but she was apparently engrossed in comparing tops.

I felt self-conscious and strange as I walked to catch the bus, as if I was being filmed. I adopted a vague smile and hummed softly to myself. Weird behaviour, yes, but it stopped the horrible traitorous tears that were yet again pricking the backs of my eyes.

On the packed bus I miraculously found a seat. I called Donna. She and Cass hadn't always seen eye to eye, ever since a couple of years before when Donna had told her to her face that Adam was a cheating wanker and only a sap would stay with him. They'd had a massive row, which ended with Cass in floods of tears and Donna storming off in disgust. They'd made up soon enough – Donna had apologized and Cass had accepted it – but there was still an atmosphere. So, yes, phoning Donna wasn't in the Top 10 of Nice Things To Do, but Cass hadn't been very nice to me.

As always, she answered almost straight away. 'Hey, girlfriend. Wait a sec . . .' I heard vague clattering noises over the rumble of the bus. 'Sorry, just putting the chips in the oven.' Donna and her dad shared cooking duties, which had the power to make me feel very useless. I didn't even know how to bake a potato. 'Good shopping?' she continued.

'Not really,' I said. 'That's what I was phoning about actually . . . Cass went all weird.'

'Oh yes?' That got her attention. I could picture her leaning against the worktop in the tiny kitchen, opening and shutting the washing-machine door with her toe.

'Yeah. I was just telling her about Joe and stuff, and she basically told me she didn't want to hear it.'

There was a pause at Donna's end. 'Oh.'

My stomach clenched. I was getting the impression I'd been the subject of distinctly non-favourable group discussion. But, ever the ostrich, I carried on regardless. 'Like, how many times have I sat and listened to her go on about Adam when he's been unfaithful?'

Donna sniffed. 'Yeah. See, thing is, babes, most of the time she doesn't talk about Adam. But Joe is literally all you ever talk about.'

I scratched my eyelid and flicked my hair out of my eyes, although my eye wasn't itchy and my hair was fine.

'. . . Like, have you even asked me how I am? Do you remember the last time you actually asked any of us anything about our lives?' she went on. Even though she couldn't see me, my face was burning. I could feel my pulse in my ears. Donna said, 'Look, I know you hate confrontation, but that doesn't mean you're always right . . .' She softened her tone a bit. 'Seriously, Sar, we love you, but you've got to snap out of this Joe thing. We want the old Sarah back.'

I cleared my throat. 'I'm sorry you think I've been neglecting you . . . Really sorry, in fact. But I don't think you will get the old Sarah back . . .' I took a slow breath. I was feeling braver now, if only because I didn't think I had anything more to lose. 'Whether you and the others like it or not, I've met someone that I really like . . . I can't always be boring, dependable Sarah just because it suits you.' I took my phone away from my ear. Donna was speaking, but I didn't want to hear any more. I pressed End Call and tucked my phone into my bag, then faced the front and clenched my hands in my lap. I just prayed that the boys still liked me.

I couldn't eat breakfast the next morning. I thought about pretending I had a migraine and staying in bed, but I figured I had to face the girls sometime, so it might as well be today. And I didn't want them thinking I was avoiding them. I had nothing to be ashamed of.

Even so, I waited till the last possible minute before leaving for school. I could miss registration for one day. I texted Ollie to say I'd overslept and could he tell Paul I'd gone to the loo.

He pinged back, 'No probs xx,' and I felt slightly better. Seemed at least Ollie was still on my side. And first period was double French, which meant I wouldn't see the girls till lunchtime. Feeling slightly better, I managed to force down a couple of pieces of toast and Marmite.

*

French was listening comprehension, which took all my concentration and meant I couldn't talk to Ollie anyway. I felt exhausted by the end of the lesson, but at least I'd not thought about anything except Mme Rochelle's trip to Paris with her two children, Pierre and Delphine, for the past hour. I wearily shrugged on my coat and picked up my bag.

'All right, flower?' asked Ollie. 'You look sad.' And to my horror my eyes instantly filled with tears. 'Oh no, McSarey. What's wrong?' He put his arm round me and I buried my face in his shoulder. 'C'mon,' he said, leading me out of the room. 'You've got a free now, right?' I nodded into the thick knitted fabric of his jumper. It smelled of washing powder. 'Well, I was going to bunk off music anyway. We can be miserable together.'

I lifted my head. 'Why are *you* miserable?'

He looked down at me briefly and smiled. 'I'm not really.'

We ended up walking around the park near school. It was just what I needed. It was the kind of damp autumn day that somehow reminds you of brisk walks followed by tea and toast in cosy kitchens, rather than low clouds and chilled bones.

Ollie tucked my hand through his arm. 'So, what's up?'

I watched the mulchy leaves leaving wet marks on my boots. 'It's nothing. Probably quite boring.'

'Shut up,' said Ollie amiably. 'I wouldn't have asked if I didn't want to know.'

So I told him everything. It felt brilliant to just come out with it, not to feel as if I had to edit in case I was being boring or try-hard or boasting, or whatever it was that the girls didn't like. When I'd finished, Ollie was quiet for a while, but it wasn't an ominous quiet like it had been with Cass and Donna. It was a thoughtful silence, as if he was letting my words find their place in the world.

'Poor old you,' he said, at last. 'What a bugger.'

I laughed mirthlessly and nodded. 'Yup.'

'Obviously I don't have a single piece of useful advice for you. I know jack about relationships. Especially girl relationships.' He shook his head as if in bemusement at the weirdness that is girl interaction. I knew what he meant. We walked in companionable silence again for a while.

'There is one thing that worries me . . . more than anything else, I mean,' I said at last, after five minutes of weighing up whether or not to say it.

'Go on.'

I bit my lip. This was it. I'd barely even asked myself this question: I didn't dare. 'Does Joe want to be with me? As in . . . be my boyfriend?' The word sounded babyish coming from me, like in primary school when you have a boyfriend for an afternoon, force him to play weddings, then release him back into the wild before moving on to the next game.

But Ollie didn't seem to think it did. He stopped walking and scratched his nose. 'I dunno, flower . . . He should do. You're lovely.' He grinned at me and I smiled back, grateful. 'But, if you really want to know what I think . . . ?' I nodded. 'I think maybe by now he'd have given you a bit more of a hint than he has done . . .' He looked like he was going to say something else, but he left it there.

I kicked at a tree trunk. 'That's what I was afraid of.'

Ollie started walking again. 'But, hey, that's just my opinion. What do I know?'

I didn't say anything, and we walked back to school in silence.

16

I couldn't avoid the girls forever, so off I went to the canteen at lunchtime, my heart in my throat and my stomach in knots.

But, when I got there, only Jack and Rich were at our table. I knew Ollie had gone to the music room to find out what he'd missed during our walk, but where were Donna, Cass and Ashley? I swallowed hard. It couldn't be a coincidence. I sat down and started unwrapping my sandwich. 'Where are the girls?' I asked casually.

Jack looked at Rich, who rolled his eyes and tutted, 'They're over there.' He nodded behind me towards the back of the canteen, where all the Year Sevens and Eights sit. I twisted round in my seat. Yep, there were my friends, on a table surrounded by small people. I turned back and tried to feel angry. This was ridiculous. You didn't gang up on each other at our age. But to be honest I felt exactly the same as I did when I was a kid, which is to say sick. And I was going to cry. Again. I angrily rubbed my eyes and tore a bite out of my sandwich.

'Sarah . . .' started Rich.

'It's OK.' I scratched my nose and carried on eating.

But he went on: 'For what it's worth, we're staying out of it.'

Jack nodded. 'We wouldn't let them tell us what's going on – as far as we're concerned it's nothing to do with us.'

The boys looked at me earnestly, and I couldn't help smiling at their serious faces. 'Thanks, guys, you're lovely.'

Rich cleared his throat. 'But . . . y'know, if *you* wanted to tell us . . .' He waggled his eyebrows suggestively.

I shrugged. 'To be honest, I'm not sure myself. They're pissed off with me for talking about Joe, I know that. But it's like, why am I not allowed to talk about him when they go on about their love-slash-sex lives as much as they want?'

Rich leant back in his chair. 'I'm with you, babes . . . Although, you have been a teeny bit obsessed lately.'

Jack laughed. 'Yeah, Joe's like the invisible man.' He put on a growly Hollywood movie trailer voice: 'He rules her life, yet no one has ever seen him . . .' He grinned at me, but then looked stricken when he saw my expression. 'Shit, sorry, Sarah. It was just a joke.'

'No, that's fine. You're entitled to your opinion.' I pushed back my chair and stood up.

'Sar, please,' said Jack, trying to pull me down by my top. 'C'mon, I'm really sorry.'

'Yeah, lighten up, dude,' smiled Rich.

I tried to smile back. 'You're right. I'm just a bit over-sensitive at the moment.' I picked up my coat and bag. 'I really do have to go.' I shot a quick glance in the direction of the girls. Cass caught my eye, said something to the other two, then stood up and beckoned me over. I mouthed, *Sorry*, and tapped the space on my wrist where a watch would have been if I had one, then hurried out of the canteen. They were having a laugh if they thought I'd put up with being summonsed to their little court of justice.

The music room was quiet when I got there. Some lower-school kid wearing headphones was on one of the computers, fiddling around with a music program, but I couldn't see Ollie. Then he knocked on the window of one of the soundproof booths.

Two minutes, he mouthed, holding up two fingers.

I smiled and nodded, and sat down to wait for him. I checked my phone. No messages. Mimi had updated her Facebook status: 'I win!!' Pfft. How very modest.

The door of Ollie's booth opened and he stuck his head out. 'Sorry, flower . . . What can I do for you?'

I smiled. 'Just came to say hello.'

'Oh. Right . . .' He glanced back into the booth. 'Well, always got time for you, McSarey.' He got a chair and parked it next to mine.

'So. How'd it go?' he asked. 'All friends again?'

I shook my head and told him about Ashley, Donna and Cass taking themselves off to a different table, but left out the stuff with Rich and Jack. I didn't want to put him in an awkward position. And, let's be honest, I didn't want him to side with them.

When I'd finished my sorry tale he kind of goggled at me in shocked bemusement. 'Shit, man. Girls are mental . . . No offence.'

I inclined my head. 'None taken.'

'So, what happens now?'

I sucked my teeth. 'No idea. They wanted to talk to me just now, but . . . I dunno. I didn't want to jump when they said jump, y'know?'

'Well, I'm just a boy and everything so obviously don't quote me on this, but wouldn't it be better just to have it out with them? I don't mean, like, girlie scratch-fight –' he paused to gaze dreamily into the middle distance – 'mmm, girlie scratch-fight . . .' I thumped him and he laughed, grabbing his arm in mock agony. 'But seriously. Just tell 'em straight.'

I sighed. 'I know. But what if they talk about me afterwards?'

Ollie looked at me through heavy eyelids. 'Sweetheart, they're girls. They are going to talk about you. Even I know that. It doesn't mean anything. Accept it and move on.'

I leant into him, nudging him with my shoulder. 'You're quite wise really, aren't you, Ols?'

He interlocked his fingers, turned his hands inside out and stretched his arms in front of him. 'You've only just realized?'

My phone vibrated a text alert and I leapt out of my seat to grab my bag, but it was just spam from some hair salon I'd been to once over a year before. Shit. I hated spam texts.

'Bad news?' asked Ollie.

I threw the phone back into my bag. 'No. Just not what I was expecting.'

'Right . . . Anyway, I'd better get back to it.' He slapped his knees and stood up. 'You're OK though?' he said, seriously.

I gave him a hug. 'I'm fine. Thanks, Ollie.'

He hugged me back. He was kind of broad and solid – really different from Joe's slenderness. 'Anytime, flower.' He went back into his sound booth and closed the door, then tapped on the window and mouthed, *Talk to them!* He accompanied this with ridiculous sign language culminating in twirly finger to side of head. I laughed and gave him an exaggerated double thumbs-up. He responded with a huge cheesy wink then turned away. Still smiling, I made my way to English, where I apologized to Rich for being a drama queen. Of course, being a boy, he'd almost forgotten it ever happened in the first place. Now all I had to do was sort it out with the girls.

That night, in my room, I phoned Donna. She was the only one I genuinely felt bad about.

'Hey.' Her voice was neutral, which was not necessarily a good sign. She did a pretty good line in quiet-but-dangerous.

I knew what I had to say. 'Donna, I'm really sorry. I shouldn't have hung up on you.'

'You're right, you shouldn't . . .' She paused, and my stomach clenched, but then she said, 'But it's OK. To be honest it was nice to see you standing up for yourself for once.'

I closed my eyes and smiled with relief. 'Great. Thanks, Don.'

'But you need to speak to Cass,' she continued. 'Leaving her in the lurch like that was low. She was really hurt, Sar.'

Now I wasn't smiling. In fact her words had flipped some internal switch and all at once I was livid. 'I didn't bloody leave her in the lurch – she practically told me to go!' I was nearly shouting. 'And what about *her* hurting *my* feelings by practically refusing to even LOOK at me?'

'Oh yes. Sorry, Sarah, I forgot. It's always about you,' said Donna, her voice like ice.

I was almost crying with frustration. How could someone who was supposed to be my friend get me so wrong? I was still working out how to respond without bursting into tears, when Donna said, 'I'm going now. Bye.'

I looked at the display on my phone. Call Ended. Just because she'd said goodbye didn't mean she hadn't hung up on me. 'Fuck you, Donna,' I said out loud. Now what? I wasn't going to call Cass. She could piss off too, with her hurt feelings. What a pile of horseshit. So I tried Ash.

'Sarah, I'm on the phone to Donna. Can I call you back?'

Shit.

'Yep. Speak to you in a bit.' But I knew she wouldn't, not after speaking to Donna, so I sent her a text instead.

> Ash I'm sorry things
> rubbish at the mo. Hope
> all ok with us? X

Really, her only beef with me was that I'd had a row with her best friend. All I could do was hope that Ash's unconventional attitude to life meant that she'd see that as none of her business. But I wasn't hopeful. She might eschew shoes and want to sleep with a girl, but underneath it all Ashley was as conventional as the rest of us. Always wanting to be different was basically just following a different kind of rule book IMHO.

I sat at my desk and logged on to my PC while I waited for Ash to get back to me. I hadn't told anyone, least of all my parents, but I'd been thinking about changing my uni choice. Depending on my grades I was planning to apply to do history of art at respected universities like Manchester and Leeds, but I was seriously considering adding Joe's uni as well. Joe was in his final year, but he'd told me he was thinking about staying on to do an MA. Everything was perfect when we were together, so it made sense for us to go to the same place, especially now I seemed to be losing all my friends.

My dad would die laughing (after he'd finished ranting) if he knew I was considering applying to do politics, even if it was joined with art history. He was always going on about how astounding it was that an intelligent person like me could be so ignorant of what's going on in the world, and what *are* they teaching you at that school of yours. And so on. Blah blah.

But I wasn't scared of a bit of hard work. If it meant I had to start actually watching the news rather than turning over to the music channels as soon as I heard Big Ben's bongs, so be it. And, anyway, London was far closer to Brighton than either of my original uni choices. Mum and Dad would be pleased about that, at least. I was pretty hopeful of my chances, too. Joe's uni didn't have the same reputation as Manchester or Leeds: I knew they'd want far lower grades. Maybe they'd even give me an unconditional offer. Not that I'd necessarily definitely take them up on it if they did. I was just looking into it.

Which reminded me. I left another voicemail asking Joe to let me know what train he'd be on.

I clicked on Firefox and logged on to my email. Nothing, just some spam promising me 'an extra 6 inches to make her scream!!!!' Ash had once replied to one of those emails: 'Dear Sir/Madam, I am female and therefore not a possessor of a penis. Please refrain from bothering me with your sicko fake product. Best of luck with your future endeavours in the genital-enlargement market. Yours, Ashley (girl).' We'd thought it was hilarious at the time, but then Ash was bombarded with literally hundreds of similar spam messages, so we didn't do that again.

As if she knew I was thinking about her, Ashley chose that exact moment to reply to my text. By phoning me. My stomach lurched, but I answered the call straight away, before I had time to chicken out.

'Hey, Ash, how are you?' Even to my own ears my voice sounded false: too hammy and bright.

'Not bad . . . I heard what happened with Donna.' It was impossible to tell which way this was going to go. Ash sounded monotone at the best of times.

'Hmm,' I mumbled warily.

'For what it's worth, I'm kind of with her on this one.'

What a surprise. Not. I said nothing.

'You have been a bit . . . single-minded recently,' she continued. 'Like, there are more important things in life than chasing a boy, especially one who's as flaky as Joe.'

'He's not that flaky,' I protested. 'He's just busy.'

Ash sighed, her breath crackling in my ear. 'You're missing the point, babes. We're worried about you, and we miss the old you. You're no fun any more.'

'Wow. Harsh.' And then, before I could stop myself, I added, 'What about Devon?'

'What about Devon?' said Ash coldly. Then, before I could answer: 'Shit, Sarah. I'm grateful for what you did – I'll never forget it, actually – but it doesn't give you the right to be a crap friend.'

Did her voice break on those last two words? I swallowed the knot of confusion, anger and hurt that was lodged in my throat.

'I don't want to be a crap friend,' I said, my voice wobbling. 'I want us to be the way we were.'

'So do I, babes,' said Ash. 'But, until you ditch all this Joe stuff, that's not going to happen.'

I picked at a thread on my jeans. 'In that case, I don't think there's anything more to say.'

I ended the call and flopped back on my bed, letting my phone clatter to the floor. So that was that. I'd lost my three best friends. The calm way we'd ended it almost made it worse. At least with a blazing row you can blame the heat of the moment. But this moment had no heat. It was chilly, and menacing, like in the middle of a long winter that feels like it's never going to end.

When I woke up I was in my pyjamas and under the covers. I fervently hoped that I'd done it myself, half asleep, and that my mum hadn't undressed me. Groggily I leant over the side of the bed and groped for my phone. Using its display as a torch, I swept it around my room. Clothes everywhere. I lay back down again, relieved. No way Mum wouldn't have folded my clothes after she'd taken them off me. Ugh. Perish the thought. Ash and her mum were always parading about naked. They never even locked the bathroom door. In fact it didn't even have a lock, which meant I only ever used the loo if I was really, really desperate. But that wasn't for me. My naked body was for my eyes only. And Joe's, of course.

Ashley. Joe. I covered my eyes with the back of my hand. Why did life have to be so complicated? I checked the time: just gone midnight. I needed to hear a friendly voice, and I knew Ollie was always late to bed. I texted him:

You still up??

And seconds later he rang back.

'What's up?' he said, his voice thick with sleep.

'Oh shit, sorry, Ollie. I didn't mean to wake you. Don't worry about it. I'll talk to you at school.'

''S'all right. I'm awake now. What's the problem?'

I coughed. 'Well. Nothing really. I just wanted to talk.'

He paused. 'D'you know what time it is?'

'I know. I just thought you might be up . . . Sorry.' I closed my eyes. I couldn't do anything right.

I heard the sound of bedsprings. 'Look, whatever it is, don't worry about it. Go to sleep, and in the morning you'll have, like, a clearer perspective.'

'Thanks, Ollie, I knew you'd make me feel better.'

I looked at my ceiling stars. One of them had come loose and was hanging precariously.

'Yeah,' he said wearily. 'Look, flower, it's late . . .'

I bit my lip. 'I know. You're right. I should never have called you. I was taking advantage. I'll see you at school.' I thought I heard him start to say something else, but I ended the call.

When I woke up six hours later, my phone was still in my hand.

I spent the next two days in bed. I didn't want to see anyone – what was the point? – and I couldn't dredge up any kind of enthusiasm for the French subjunctive, mid-twentieth-century art or even *Jane Eyre*. So I told my parents I had a migraine and settled down to my new life as a social recluse. Ollie called me twice and Rich and Jack both tried once, but I ignored them. Everything that came out of my mouth seemed to be wrong, so it was probably best to keep it shut. Needless to say, not a word from Cass, Donna or Ashley. I texted Joe three times and called him twice, but didn't leave voicemails. Not a word from him, either.

And then on Friday afternoon, after a day and a half of reaching new levels of hair-greasiness, PJ-wearingness and needing-a-showeryness, I got a text.

I was so monged through lack of activity that I

didn't even move from my position on the sofa watching . . . I don't even remember what – probably something tragic like *Everybody Loves Raymond* – when my phone chirruped. It wasn't until the next ad break when I hauled my arse into the kitchen to get another bowl of cereal that I saw my phone on the table and remembered the text. Funny how these things happen when you're least prepared. My pulse quickened when I saw it was from Joe. I smiled. About bloody time. I clicked on the button to open the message.

> Sorry babes, can't make
> the party after all. V busy
> with work, exams, etc.
> You know the score Xx

I think I was beginning to get a pretty good idea of the score, yes. It went something like this: I wait ages for Joe to arrange to meet up; he eventually arranges to meet up; I get excited; he blows me out. It was no way to live, and definitely no way to conduct a relationship. Letting my vaguely whiffy carcass flop into the nearest chair, I read the message again. Was this the response I'd been waiting nearly a week for? A totally lame brush-off?

Suddenly it was like I was looking down on myself from above. I hadn't showered or changed my clothes in nearly two days. I'd alienated my friends and wasted forty-eight hours of my life watching shitty telly and feeling sorry for myself, and now Joe – the cause of all this grief – had casually blown me off after nearly a week of radio silence. I'd had enough.

If Joe couldn't come to me, I'd go to him. If we had any kind of a future together, he needed to sort himself out. Even if I had to make him.

17

As if I'd been conserving all my energy for this moment, I leapt into action. I showered, put on my favourite outfit – the jeans and big jumper – and dried my hair. I bunged some overnight stuff in a bag, brushed two days' worth of fur off my teeth, swilled with mouthwash, and I was ready to go.

I sat in front of a Post-It for a minute, tapping my pen on my teeth and wondering what to tell my parents, then thought, *Sod it*, and wrote: 'Gone to London. Will call you later. xxx'. Honesty was the best policy and all that. Anyway, they both had meetings after work. By the time they saw the note, I'd be on the train.

It was nearly dark when I got to the station, and the adrenalin rush had all but disappeared. The whole idea was beginning to seem ridiculous, but I forced myself to buy a ticket. I couldn't see how else I was going to see Joe. And face to face was the only way I could be sure of pinning him down and making him sort it out.

On the train I found a seat and purposefully opened my book. A couple of girls I vaguely recognized from school – Year Tens I think – walked past. One of them was saying, 'Can you believe her?' and the other one shook her head and sucked her teeth. I went scarlet, like an idiot. I don't know in what reality they could have been talking about me. They didn't even know me.

I splayed my book page-down across my lap and used the dark window as a mirror to stare at a couple sitting in the seats across the aisle. They weren't much older than me. She had her legs thrown over his and was resting her head on his shoulder. He murmured something to her and she laughed and reached up to stroke his cheek. She was wearing a ring on her fourth finger. It was a solid band with a diamond – or whatever – kind of embedded in it. It was exactly the sort of ring I'd choose. I thought: what must it be like to be her? To be loved by someone so much that they want everyone to know they're going to be with you forever? I literally couldn't imagine. All I knew was that I thought I might hate that woman. It's not like I was looking to get married – that would be stupid. I just wanted to be wanted.

I narrowed my eyes as the woman idly turned the ring with her thumb and smiled. Smug bitch. As if she could hear my thoughts she looked into her

window and we made strange, reflective eye-con-
tact. She stared at me for a brief second then
carelessly looked away. Nothing to see here. I refo-
cused my eyes so I wasn't looking at her, but at the
darkness and shadows of the world outside. The
train bumped gently on the track as it sped towards
London, its muffled *dugga dugga* like I was hearing it
under water. I had a sneaking suspicion I might be
turning invisible.

The train got into Victoria station at just gone eight.
The place was packed with commuters on their way
home for the weekend. I imagined welcoming lit win-
dows, a bottle of wine on ice, Ikea double beds
covered in throws and pillows, maybe a sheepskin
rug on the floor. Couples waking up together in the
morning, reading the Saturday papers in bed, having
sex . . .

Being seventeen and still at school suddenly
seemed so stifling I could hardly breathe. Coursework, exams, watching Friday-night TV with my
parents and Daniel . . . it was kill-me-now tedious. I
wanted to be like Mimi, basically. Not a total bitch-ho
from hell, of course, but at college, away from home,
free to be whoever I wanted to be. I wondered if the
way she was had been a conscious decision. Like,
every night before bed she looked in the mirror and

chanted, 'I am confident, and groomed, and have silky hair like Kate Middleton. People want to be my friend.'

Or probably it just comes naturally, I thought gloomily.

I tried to shake Mimi from my mind. This was not about her, it was about Joe. I ran down the escalator to the Tube platform. The northbound platform was rammed and the digital display thing blank. I hovered outside the platform entrance. I couldn't understand how people weren't toppling on to the line, it was so packed. A tannoy announcement informed me that due to signal failure in the Seven Sisters area there were severe delays on the Victoria line. Brilliant. I only needed to get to Oxford Circus – from there I could get the Bakerloo line all the way to Kensal Green, where Joe lived. I ran back up the escalator to ground level to look for a bus map. It told me I needed a 73, which arrived just as I got to the stop. I edged my way down the packed bus until someone got out of their seat just as I was passing, and I sat down gratefully. Two bits of luck in a row: I took it as a good sign.

We'd been juddering and bouncing along for a few minutes when the woman next to me said, 'Excuse me?' She was pretty old with really short steel-grey hair and bright blue eyes. She was wearing a bottle-green velvet coat (which I so would have worn myself, if Ash hadn't already bagsied the vampire-coat-wearing slot in our friendship group. And then I remembered I wasn't in her friendship group any more). She peered over half-moon glasses and smiled. The woman didn't fit any kind of description of axe-murdering rapist, so I felt safe enough answering her, even on a London bus. I smiled politely, like the good girl I am.

'Yes?'

'I hope you don't mind my asking, but do you go to Woodside High?'

I gawped at her. 'Uh, yeah . . . How did you know?'

She pointed to the lower-school prefect badge I'd pinned to my rucksack in an attempt at ironic retro chic (or at least that's how the magazine where I got the idea put it).

'I used to teach there! Gosh, fifteen years ago now.'

'Really? Wow! I bet it's changed a lot since then,' I said lamely.

She nodded enthusiastically. 'Oh, I expect it has.' She put her hand on my arm. 'What a wonderful coincidence meeting you!' She beamed at me and I smiled back. What else could I do?

'I'm Kate,' she said, and offered her hand. I shook it and told her my name. 'So what brings you to London, Sarah?' she asked, folding her hands in her lap as if she was settling down for a chat. I didn't mind. I liked her.

'I'm going to see my boyfriend.' I tried on the word for size. It felt strange and a bit false, but I could get used to it. 'He goes to uni here.'

'Ah. Did he used to go to Woodside too?'

I shook my head. 'We met on holiday actually.'

The woman leant back towards the window as if she was examining me anew. 'Wow! A holiday romance that's lasted. Well done you!'

I smiled weakly. 'Thanks.'

'So tell me, is Greta Parsons still teaching history?'

I shook my head, and she proceeded to reel off a list of teachers, some who were still at school, most who weren't. It would have been a nice way to pass the journey, if I wasn't still thinking about the holiday romance comment.

At Oxford Circus I got off the bus, along with almost everyone else, and joined the throngs trudging down the stairs to the Tube station. There were no problems with the Bakerloo line, I was relieved to see, and I got a seat straight away. But as the Tube drew closer to Kensal Green the knot in my stomach got tighter. It wasn't as if I was surprising Joe – I'd texted to let him know. But still. I was nervous. A lot rode on this visit. I closed my eyes and imagined him opening the door, giving me his saucy lopsided smile and silently pulling me inside and upstairs to his room, where I'd barely have time to take off my coat before he drew me down on to the bed with him. He would take a few seconds to look at me, to take me in. He would trace round my mouth with his fingers and gently kiss my eyelids, then he'd slowly remove my clothes before tenderly making love to me. Afterwards he would hold me in his arms and tell me he loved me.

Positive thinking. If you want something badly enough, it will happen. Yeah, right.

I opened my eyes. *Don't hope for miracles*, I told myself sternly. *Just be happy if he's pleased to see you and willing to talk. That's all you can ask.*

I didn't know why I was worrying so much. Despite his crapness at keeping in touch, Joe had never been anything other than happy to see me. That was the trouble: we were the kind of couple who needed to be together.

By the time I was walking to his house from the station, I felt better. I was here now. I'd just take it as it came. But as I turned the corner into his street it struck me that he might not even be home. I supposed Rav and Ben could let me wait in his room, but what if they'd all gone out together? How long would I wait outside his house before I gave up and skulked home? What if they'd gone out for the night? They might not be back till, like, two or three in the morning. But as I approached his house I could see the light in his room was on. I stood for a moment just out of sight and took a moment to calm myself. Then I strode confidently up the path and rang the doorbell.

18

One of the girls from the pub opened the door. Mara/Lara or – what was the other one? Rosie. Anyway, not Mimi, thank God. Whoever-it-was looked at me blankly for a second, then smirked as she recognized me. 'Can I help you?'

I flashed her a brilliant smile. 'Hi! Is Joe in . . .?' I peered round as if I was expecting him to materialize at any second. She moved to block my view, then apparently thought better of it and stepped aside. She smiled sweetly. 'Yeah, course. Come in.'

'Oh. Thanks.' I moved past her into the hallway. It was weird being in the house with her.

'He's in his room,' she said unnecessarily. I was already going upstairs – it hadn't occurred to me that he'd be anywhere else. It was the only room in the house we'd ever been in together, although the thought didn't strike me till later.

I stopped outside his closed door. I could hear music coming from inside. I knocked, tentatively first, then louder. When there was still no answer I turned the handle and went in.

The light was so dim I could hardly see anything. There was a lava lamp next to his bed, which I'd never seen before. Deep red blobs floating languorously to the top then flopping down again. It was kind of mesmerizing. I couldn't see Joe – I thought he must be in the bathroom, but then a sound came from the bed. I looked over and frowned at the mass of light hair hanging over the end of the mattress. Joe didn't have hair like that. Then, as my eyes adjusted to the light, I finally understood. I gasped and bolted from the room. I stood outside for a second, blood pounding in my ears. Without knowing what else to do, I ran into the bathroom and locked the door.

The hair had belonged to Mimi. And her legs were wrapped round Joe's back.

My breath came in shallow gasps. I dragged my fingers down my cheeks. What the hell was I going to do? I looked at the bathroom window, but there was no way I'd fit through there. Anyway, it was a straight drop down two floors into a paved alley. Then I shrieked as someone banged on the door.

'Sarah, I know that's you.' He knocked again. 'Come on, open the door.' It was Joe's voice, but not the one I remembered. It was cold and hard.

I unlocked the door and barged through, knocking Joe to one side. He caught my arm, but I shook him off and hurtled, head down, towards the stairs.

'What the hell did you think you were doing coming here anyway?' he yelled after me. 'I told you I didn't want anything serious . . . Sarah!'

At the top of the stairs the sight of Mimi leaning against the wall – her smooth, bare legs crossed casually at the ankle, one of Joe's T-shirts barely covering her arse – made me stop short. She waved her fingers at me. 'Bye then!' I swallowed the desire to spit in her face and skidded down the stairs, wrenched open the front door and ran.

'Please let there be a train, please let there be a train,' I keened through gritted teeth as I careered across the road to the station. But there was no sign of one, and wouldn't be for ten minutes, according to the display. I walked to the far end of the platform and pressed myself against the wall. I hadn't cried like this since I was little. Noisy, racking sobs that made my teeth chatter. 'But I love him' kept running through my head. As if that could ever have been enough.

The train rattled through the stations, but I was oblivious. I felt disembodied. That girl with the puffy face and snail trails up her sleeve wasn't me. It was some other stupid, delusional cow. Whoever came up with 'It's better to have loved and lost than never to have loved at all' was (a) talking bollocks and (b) assuming the love went both ways. Did I have any right to complain about losing something I never had in the first place? Because I'd finally realized what everyone else must have known all along. Joe didn't love me, and he never had. He never would.

The thought triggered another crying explosion, forcing out a giant snot bubble. Lack of tissues meant I had to bend down and wipe my face on the underside of my jumper. Not for the first time I was grateful that strangers don't talk to each other in London. Except for that woman Kate on the bus. I remembered her comment about holiday romances. Even a complete stranger could tell that Joe didn't give a toss about me. And I'd even looked into going to his uni! Thank God nothing had come of that.

I pulled at my hair and made a strange buzzing sound from moaning through bared teeth.

'Excuse me, is there anything I can do?'

I squinted through swollen eyes at a woman in a suit. She was standing in front of me holding on to the overhead bar for support, her forehead creased with concern. I must have looked a state: crying and rocking and making weird animalistic noises. She was quite brave, when you think about it. I shook my head, and, when she still didn't go away, I croaked, 'I'm OK.'

'Are you sure?'

I gave her a look, and she went back to her seat.

There wasn't anything anyone could do. Least of all me.

I started crying all over again when I finally arrived back in Brighton. Cry me a river? I was the bloody Nile. Denial is not just a river in Egypt, as my dad would say. Ha ha.

It was nearly midnight, and the centre of town was buzzing with couples, draped all over each other like adverts for their own sex lives. I remembered my public display of affection with Joe at Victoria. It meant nothing to him, therefore maybe it meant nothing to all these people. *So you can just smug off*, I thought bitterly as another couple passed by, their hands in each other's bum pockets.

I stood outside the station, snivelling and wondering what to do. I couldn't go home. Mum and Dad had left two increasingly irate messages on my phone. I'd texted to say I was fine – that I was staying with Ashley's cousin again – but something told me that wouldn't be enough. And obviously I couldn't call any of the girls. Rich and Jack? That would be too weird. I sighed. It had to be Ollie. I needed him. He'd understand.

And luckily the sound of his voice when he answered the phone unleashed torrents of fresh tears, so he was too busy feeling sorry for me to feel used. (Anyway, I wasn't using him. He was now my closest friend. Ollie: my best friend! The thought was startling, like watching something on the news and realizing it happened in the next street.) I asked if I could stay at his. He said yes – he even offered to come and get me, but I told him I needed the air. Which I did, but more than that I needed to sort my face out. I'd cried so much I must have looked like I'd had some kind of allergic episode. I went into a McDonald's that was too busy for anyone to notice I was using the loos without buying anything, and spent five minutes splashing my face with cold water and applying liberal amounts of tinted moisturizer. It helped, a bit. I still looked hideous, but who cared?

By the time I got to Ollie's – he lived a good twenty-minute walk from the station – I'd composed myself enough to say 'hi' to his parents, who were watching late-night telly in the sitting room. Obviously not early-to-bed types, then. I'd hoped I wouldn't have to see them, but his mum just smiled at me sympathetically and didn't try to do small talk, so he must have told her I needed a place to stay. His parents were pretty relaxed about him having girls over, anyway, or how else could he maintain his impressive record as everyone's favourite commitment-phobe?

He led me into the kitchen, which was cosy and

still done out in the orange pine it always had been. He pulled a chair out from under the table. 'Take the weight off.'

I smiled gratefully, too exhausted to make conversation. I looked around while he made the tea. Nothing much had changed since we were tiny. The fridge was still covered with Ollie-phernalia: old drawings, school notices, attendance certificates. Poking out at the bottom was a yellowing piece of paper with a felt-tip drawing of two big stick figures and one little one. They were holding hands with long, spindly arms. At the bottom an adult had written: 'My family, by Oliver Glazer, age 5'.

I gestured to the picture. 'Pride of place on the fridge. 'S'being an only child for you. When Dan started school I threw a fit because I thought Mum and Dad were favouring his works of art over mine.'

Ollie smiled. 'Yeah, well. Mum and Dad tried to have kids after Zac died, but they couldn't. I used to really want a brother or sister.'

My blood ran cold. I was appalled. 'I'm so sorry, Ollie. I completely forgot about Zac.' I put my head in my hands. 'Talk about self-obsessed.'

'Don't worry about it,' he said lightly, a cup of tea in each hand. 'Shall we go upstairs?' I picked up my bag and followed him up to his room, still mentally cursing myself. 'You've got the spare room,' he said.

'But come and talk to me first.' He pushed open his bedroom door with his foot and nodded for me to go in. I sat on the edge of his bed, feeling disorientated and spacey. He handed me my tea and sat down beside me.

'So. Bad day?' He took a campy slurp of tea *à la* old-lady-gossip.

I made a kind of huffy noise. Laughing without laughing. 'You could say that.' I twisted my hands in my lap and told him what had happened, and he listened without comment. 'I'm such an idiot,' I said, when I'd finished. I put my head in my hands. 'I'm so *stupid*.'

Ollie looked into his empty mug. 'Nah,' he said. 'You're not an idiot.'

'But everyone knew Joe didn't give a shit about me.'

He shrugged. 'We could have been wrong.' He raised his eyes to mine. 'And none of us will get any satisfaction out of being right.'

I smiled sadly. I was grateful to him for not pretending anyone ever thought there was any kind of future for me and Joe. He put his arm round me and pulled me to him. 'Come here.' I leant my head on his shoulder. 'This is a shit thing that's happened, flower. But you deserve . . . God, *so* much better than him.' He sounded almost angry. I smiled

up at him and he looked down at me, his chin
wrinkling.

And then he spoiled it all by trying to kiss me.

I leapt up like I'd been stung. 'What are you *doing*?'
   'Sorry. I'm sorry.' He looked stricken. 'Shit, Sarah.
I totally misjudged that. Please, sit down.'
   'I can't handle this.' I picked up my bag and, for the
second time that day, ran out of a boy's house in tears.
   I ran for a few minutes, then sat down on someone's garden wall, both to get my breath back and get
my head round things. Today was weird. And horrible. I had no frame of reference for today. I had never
before walked in on the boy I loved to find him grunting away on top of the person I hated most in the
world. I had never been kissed by someone I thought
was my friend. Was this what life's rich tapestry was
all about? Broken hearts and betrayal and disappointment? I'd always sneered at those girls at school who
get engaged to their boyfriends, which seemed to me
not much more than a word and an Argos ring on the
relevant finger, but suddenly I could kind of understand why they did it. It was like armour, albeit crap
armour that doesn't work. I'd only ever heard of one
of these couples actually getting married – but they
were Travellers and they always marry young.

'Oi!' An angry voice came from above me. I looked up to see an old man sticking his head out of an upstairs window. 'You going to sit there all night?'

What did he think I was going to do – snort drugs off his wall? Wearily I stood up and started walking in the direction of home, not being quite desperate or melodramatic enough to wander the streets till dawn. And anyway, it was freezing.

Mum and Dad were on me as soon I turned the key in the lock. They must have legged it out of the sitting room, the better to be all righteously angry the moment I walked in.

Mum was giving me one of her patented *Who do you think you are?* glares while my dad was practically spitting with rage. 'Where the hell have you been?' he fumed.

Wow. Original. I rolled my eyes and pushed past them to get to the stairs, but my dad grabbed my wrist. 'I don't think so.'

I let my head flop back and sighed heavily at the ceiling. I so couldn't be bothered with this. 'Look, I just want to go to bed. Can we talk in the morning?'

'No we fucking can't,' said my dad, who gets foul-mouthed when he's really angry. It's like: *I'm laying down the law, but see how I swear and therefore treat you as an equal.* Or some such bollocks.

Then my mum weighed in. 'We do NOT deserve to be treated like this. You do NOT just go out without asking – not while you're living here. Show us some BLOODY respect.'

And that was it. I'd had enough. I simply could not take them having a go at me on top of everything else today. I wrenched my arm out of my dad's grasp. 'Why don't you just PISS OFF!' I yelled and, for the first time in my life, stormed out of the house.

'WHERE THE HELL DO YOU THINK YOU'RE GOING?' he bellowed, giving the neighbours a rare treat. I turned round at the bottom of the drive.

'I'm going to Cass's, all right? Or do you want me to write a letter requesting permission?'

My mum shot me a disgusted look. 'Let her go, Martin,' she said. 'Frankly, I can't bear to have her in the house.'

'You and me both,' I spat.

So it looked like I was going to Cass's. She only lived round the corner, or there's no way my parents would have let me go. Whether she'd let me in was another matter. I got my phone out of my bag and scrolled to Recent Calls. She was way down the list. Until last week I'd spoken to her almost every day. I clicked on her name, but she let it go to voicemail. I wasn't surprised.

'Cass, it's me . . . Please can I come over? I know it's late, and you probably hate me, but I walked in on Joe in bed with that Mimi bitch and I can't stay at home . . . or anywhere else . . .' I closed my eyes in dismay. What the hell was Ollie *thinking*? '. . . So anyway. Please call me back when you get this.'

She rang just as I got to her house.

'Where are you?'

'Outside.'

'I'm coming down.'

I don't know what I expected, but if it was a joyful reunion with tearful promises never to argue again, I was wrong. Cass opened the door and just stood, kind of warily watching me. I honestly couldn't remember what we were fighting about. Were we even fighting at all? Like, I hadn't even spoken to her since I'd left her in town – it was Donna who'd told me she was upset. Putting my bag down on the step, I took a couple of steps towards her and put my arms round her. It was a massive gamble. If she'd not returned the hug I think I would have shrivelled up and died, right there on the doorstep. I'd have died of shit-day. But she didn't. She hugged me back. Cue reunion.

'Why are we even fighting?' she asked, laugh-crying into my shoulder.

'I was thinking the exact same thing.' I stood back and looked her in the eye. 'Cass, if I've been a crap friend, I'm really sorry. I didn't mean to be.'

She shook her head earnestly. 'No, I've been crap too. Let's just forget it. It was a ridiculous moment in an otherwise model friendship and in thirty years we'll laugh about it over tea and pineapple upside-down cake.'

I laughed. Pineapple upside-down cake was like our code for being old and senile, after Mrs Fieldhouse, our ancient Year Seven food-tech teacher who was obsessed with it. We must have made it four times in one year. 'Nature's healer, children!' she used to say, brandishing a tin of pineapple rings. 'All that lovely bromelain!' (Fair play to her, though – if bromelain ever came up in Trivial Pursuit, we were laughing.)

Upstairs in Cass's bedroom I put on my PJs – Cass had already donned her pristine night attire – and we got into bed. She had a white wooden double bed with crisp white covers and a giant canvas print of her and Adam taking a bite out of the same apple above it. Cass didn't Blu-Tack her posters to the wall; she framed them and hung them properly. Her desk was immaculate, her PC monitor and keyboard free of dust and bits of old food, her floorboards shiny and her rug covered in fresh Hoover tracks. In short, she was a true list-maker. Fastidious was her middle name, or it would have been if it hadn't actually been Marjorie (a top-secret fact only I knew – I think even Adam might have been in the dark on that one).

Cass turned out the light and we lay next to each other in the dark. It was a relief to be in a familiar situation. We'd shared this bed loads of times. There was a hard ball of grief and worry in my stomach and every time I thought about Joe, or Ollie, or Mum and Dad, I had to concentrate on not crying, but being with Cass was good.

'Do you want to talk about it?' she asked, her voice quiet.

We'd hardly said a thing to each other since the pineapple upside-down cake moment. I think Cass had been waiting to ask me about stuff under cover of darkness. She knew I hated crying in front of people, although blowing a snot balloon in a packed Tube carriage kind of puts blubbing with friends into perspective.

'I do, but can we do it in the morning?' I yawned. 'I just want to sleep.'

'Course we can.' She briefly tickled my forehead. ''Night, hon.'

I would have said goodnight back, but I couldn't. I was trying to cry soundlessly. Joe used to tickle my forehead like that.

'Sarah, honey. You OK?'

'Uh-huh.' I took a calming yet gross and mucousy breath in through my nose and out through my mouth, then gave in to the exhaustion and fell fast asleep.

19

'Sarah, honey. I've brought you a cup of tea.'

I prised apart my eyelids. Cass was leaning over me. For a split second everything was fine, then I remembered, and the whole pile of crap came tumbling down on me.

'Ugh, thanks,' I said, pushing myself up into a sitting position and taking the cup. 'What time is it?'

'Nearly ten. You've slept for almost ten hours!' She stroked my hair away from my forehead. 'How are you feeling?'

'Crap.' I took a sip of tea and closed my eyes as the hot liquid warmed me from the inside. 'But I suppose I'll live.'

Cass smiled supportively and patted my leg. 'Listen, I've called the others. We're meeting on the beach in an hour.'

I grimaced. 'How were they?'

'Yeah, fine. Don't worry about it.'

Hmm. I'd wait and see about that one. I nodded. 'OK, but I'll see you there. I have to talk to my parents.'

She stood up. 'OK. I'll leave you to get ready. Help yourself to the shower and stuff. I'll make you some toast, shall I?'

'Thanks, but I'm not hungry. I'll grab something later.'

As soon as she'd left the room I pulled on yesterday's clothes without bothering to shower, shouted a quick goodbye, and ran back round the corner to our house.

And there, swallowing my anger because I didn't want them to get any ideas about banning me from going to Ollie's bonfire party that night, I grovelled like a good 'un. I told them I'd had a huge row with the girls. *I was confused and upset. It just felt like everyone was getting at me. I'm truly sorry, it won't happen again. Blah blah.* It was a virtuoso performance, even if I do say so myself.

My dad, who doesn't bear grudges, was v. impressed with my new-found maturity and let me off instantly. My mum, who does bear grudges, was still a bit frosty. But she'd get over it. Anyway, I was allowed to go to Ollie's party, which was the main thing. I told my parents I'd get ready at Cass's but I'd be back home by midnight. Tick tick tick. All sorted.

Upstairs in my room I spent a few minutes standing in front of my wardrobe staring uninspired at the hangers of dullness that passed as my clothes, before remembering that – duh! – it was a bonfire party. Jeans, coat, scarf and hat were what I needed. And I had a gorgeous grey trilby that I loved, but hadn't worn for weeks since Joe informed me that men's hats on girls look stupid. But I knew it suited me. It was my magic hat, making my eyes look bigger and giving me cheekbones I never knew I had. I stood taller when I was wearing it, felt more confident.

Standing there, holding it in my hand, I realized what a total idiot I'd been.

I looked in the mirror on my wardrobe door and pulled an extreme *duh* face. I couldn't even entirely blame Joe. Don't get me wrong, I knew he'd been a dick. He'd totally used me for sex – and made me think he really liked me at Will's party – but he'd also told me right at the beginning that he wasn't looking for anything serious. If I hadn't constantly texted him, he'd probably have let it go. And was it his fault I never wore my hat? I didn't have to take one throw-away comment as some kind of commandment. *Thou shalt not wear men's hats if thou wants to be withst me* type thing. For all her mental bitchiness – and she was a mental bitch, I was convinced of that – I couldn't believe that Mimi would ever change anything about herself for anyone. I kicked the wardrobe door shut. It was so painful to think of Joe and Mimi together.

Like, it physically hurt. I couldn't bear it. The fact that I at least partly had myself to blame did not help, at all. In fact, it probably made it worse.

I lay on my bed and gave myself precisely five minutes to wail into my pillow. I even set the alarm on my phone. If I couldn't make the crying stop – and it seemed pretty obvious that I couldn't – then I wasn't going to let it take over my life.

Sarah was back in the saddle. Well, nearly. I had a few things to do before I galloped off into the sunset.

For once I wasn't the first to arrive. Cass, Ashley and Donna were already waiting outside The Pump Room cafe on the beach when, out of breath and apologetic, I finally got there. But they were fine with it. The universe didn't implode because I was five minutes late. Who knew? And when Donna started to say something, I interrupted. 'No, let me speak first.' She stopped, looking surprised – but not angry.

I stood tall, my hands by my sides, flicking the thumb and middle finger of each hand together as a vent for my nerves. I cleared my throat. 'You were right, I was obsessed with . . . the Joe thing.' It was hard to even say his name. 'I realize that now. And I'm really sorry if any of you felt like I was neglecting you.' I looked at each of my friends in turn: Cass smiling encouragingly, Ash nodding sagely and

Donna looking at the floor and rocking back and forth on her Uggs.

I swallowed. 'But at the same time . . . I don't think you needed to be quite so harsh with me. It's not like I was being malicious. I was just a bit . . . I dunno, naive. Anyway, it's all over now.' I blinked back fresh tears. 'And, if it's OK with you, I'd really like to forget it and move on.'

Donna wrapped me in a huge hug. 'No, babes, you're right. I'm sorry too. I hated seeing you so into him when he obviously didn't give a shit about you.' I tensed, and she quickly added, 'And maybe I was a bit jealous. Like, I haven't had a boyfriend, or anything close, in months, and there you were – man-hater Sarah – all loved up with an older man.'

My eyes went all big and round. Wow. I hadn't been expecting that. Then I felt Ashley's arms round me. 'I'm sorry too, babes. I think I got a bit freaked by the fact you'd, y'know, like saved my life and shit.'

And then Cass put her arms round all of us. 'I'm so glad we're all together again!'

We stood there for a few seconds in happy group huggage, until a bunch of lads swaggered past and one of them said, 'Dirty lezzers.' We pulled apart, giggling. Donna grabbed my face and moved her head towards me, waggling it from side to side so to the boys it would've looked like she was giving me a full-on tongue-pash.

'Oh, baby, your bosoms drive me wild with desire,' I fluted, while Ashley and Cass busied themselves with the mechanics of groping each other's arses. I didn't even know if the lads were still there. It was just so nice to be mucking about again. No drama.

A bit later on, when we were sitting in the cafe drinking hot chocolate, I told them about going to Joe's, and about finding him and Mimi together. I cried, of course, but each time I told the story it got a bit easier.

Afterwards no one said anything for a few seconds. The girls looked shell-shocked. 'God, Sarah. That's awful,' said Donna finally. 'You poor cow.' I chewed my cheek and nodded.

'I can't believe he got with that Mimi bitch,' added Ash, shaking her head. 'He has so bitten off more than he can chew. She'll eat him alive.'

Cass raised her mug. 'Nice mixing of eating metaphors there, lady.'

I thought of Mimi's Facebook status: 'I win.' Could she have been referring to Joe? It was almost flattering to think that she genuinely saw me as a threat. It seemed glaringly obvious to me now that I really never was. Joe was just out for a good time, and a school kid from Brighton was only a very small and temporary part of it. I swirled my spoon in my cup, making foam figure-of-eights, and tried not to succumb to the blackness that was threatening to suck me under.

'It'll be OK, honey,' said Cass, stroking my hair. 'You'll find someone else. Someone who deserves you.'

The events of last night came flooding back. I put my head in my hands and groaned. 'Oh God, that reminds me . . . Ollie tried to kiss me last night.'

'WHAT?!' My friends spoke as one, all now sitting bolt upright with eyes like gossip-receiving satellites.

'It was awful,' I said. 'I told him about Joe and he, like, gave me a comforting hug and then . . . oh God, he tried to kiss me.' My stomach clenched at the memory. It'd been so embarrassing. 'I couldn't handle it. I just ran away.' I peered up from under my hand. 'Like, what was he *thinking*?'

The girls looked at each other and smiled. 'Babes,' said Ash gently, 'he likes you. It's blatantly obvious.'

'No he doesn't,' I scoffed. 'He's like that with everyone. All that "flower" stuff.'

Donna laughed. 'Sarah, you dick, you're the only one he ever calls flower.' I looked sceptical, and she said, 'Think about it. Have you ever heard him say it to anyone else?' I did think about it, really hard, and

Donna was right. He called girls mate, or babes, but not flower.

'Wow. Ollie . . .' I tapped my nails on the side of my cup. 'But I'm so not his type.'

Cass rolled her eyes. 'Hello? Why do you think he's never had a proper girlfriend before? They. Weren't. His. Type.' She punctuated each word with a light punch to the side of my head.

I thought about it for a moment. 'No. Even if you're right, I don't fancy him. I can't,' I said decisively, leaning back in my chair.

'Can't? Or won't?' said Ashley, steepling her hands meaningfully.

I shrugged. 'I'm over men, that's all. I need time for myself. For you lot.' And my friends all piled on to me again in another hug. Closing my eyes and laughing as I fended off their lung-bustingly tight squeezes, I thought, *I might feel like crap, but at least I've got my friends to help me through it.* All *my friends.*

I extricated myself from the girls' grasp. 'Listen, I need to sort things out with Ollie before tonight. Will you still be here in, like, half an hour?' They looked at each other and nodded, and I bolted.

I didn't think. I just ran. Ollie had been a true friend over the last few weeks. I was a bit scared about what he might say, although I had to admit I was also kind of flattered. I'd meant it when I said was off men, but still. After everything that had happened with Joe, the idea of being fancied at all was kind of a massive relief, even if I couldn't fancy him back. But Ollie was a sweetheart, and I couldn't lose his friendship. I couldn't let him go.

He opened the door slowly, peering round it and wincing. 'Have you come to punch me in the face?'

I laughed. 'Nope, not this time.' I brushed imaginary whatever off my coat and cleared my throat. 'I've come round to say I'm sorry . . . And we're cool.' My eyes swivelled up to meet his. 'I hope?'

He opened the door fully. 'Course we are. I'm sorry too, for . . . y'know . . .' He winced again. 'Honestly, I don't know what came over me. Something in the moment, I suppose . . . Like, you're gorgeous and all, but you and me? I don't think so!' He laughed. 'Can you imagine?!'

I smiled, relief and slight disappointment battling it out inside me. Relief won, of course. 'It's fine. Seriously.'

He stepped back. 'You coming in?'

'I'd better not, the girls are waiting for me.'

Ollie beamed. 'You're all friends again!' I shrugged happily. 'Nice one. I hated to see you sad.' He smiled at me, sort of shyly. My insides clenched as he looked like he was about to say something else, but he didn't, and we kind of stood, saying nothing, for a few moments.

'Anyway, I'd better . . .' I gestured with my thumb back towards the path.

'Yeah, course . . . See you at the party. You're still coming, right?'

'Course. Wouldn't miss it.'

I was about to turn round when he said, 'Uh . . . Sarah?'

'Uh . . . Yeah?' I mimicked. Anything to keep the atmosphere light.

He ran his hand through his hair and stopped at the top of his head, his fist full of curls. I tensed as I waited for what he was going to say, rapidly trying to conjure up appropriate responses, but then he surprised me.

'I really am sorry. I was a dick for putting our friendship in jeopardy. You're so great, I'd just be gutted if I thought we couldn't carry on like we were before . . . well, before I was a dick. I honestly don't know what I was thinking. Can we try to forget it ever happened? Never speak of it again, type thing?' He bit his lip and smiled nervously.

Mentally having a go at myself for having the gall to feel disappointed when I knew I didn't want him, not really, I rested my cheek on his chest. He did brilliant hugs, I'd give him that. All strong arms and broad shoulders.

'You're the nicest boy in the whole, wide world,' I said, squeezing him.

His chest shuddered as he laughed. 'I'm glad you think so.'

I pulled back and smiled. 'See you tonight, then.'

He raised his hand in a motionless wave, and I turned and walked away.

But it was funny. He kept popping into my head as me and the girls walked along the beach that afternoon. I ignored it, though. I'd made my decision, and, anyway, I'd learned my lesson. No more zoning out to daydream about boys.

'So, Ash,' I said, linking my arm through hers. 'Any gossip?'

But she didn't answer my question, saying instead, 'It's strange, I'm not as scared of it as I'd thought I'd be.' I followed her gaze out to sea.

'Oh no, please tell me you're not wearing your cozzie under that lot.' I shot horror-film wide-eyes at her enormo-boots, skinny jeans and military cape combo, and she gave me a body shove. 'Oh yes, très amusing.' But she was smiling. 'Anyway, I don't need to, do I? I've crossed it off my list.'

We continued walking arm in arm, in companionable silence. Cass and Donna were walking slightly ahead of us, deep in conversation. If nothing else, the past few weeks' weirdness had brought the two of them closer together. I was glad.

Later that night the four of us stood outside the party, our cheeks pink from the cold and our breath making little puffs in the air. We were fashionably late, and I wasn't even bothered. I felt good. The tears were at bay, for now at least, and I was ready to enjoy myself.

And then my text alert sounded. Smiling sheepishly, I quickly checked it.

> Sarah Doesn't-like-beer,
> we need to talk. I'm free
> this weekend . . .? x

'Who's it from?' asked Cass.

I pressed the Delete button. 'No one.'

And so the four of us pushed open the front door and walked into Ollie's house. Over all the familiar faces I could see him standing in the kitchen, pouring bags of marshmallows into bowls. He caught my eye and smiled.

Don't miss the next fantastic book, coming soon in paperback and ebook:

Turn over for an exclusive extract . . .

I hardly ever came to the Year Thirteen common room. It was too busy and it smelled weird, like feet, and sandwiches that had been wrapped in clingfilm, but you could make a cup of tea for free so it was where I came when I was skint. And I *was* skint, ever since my mum had stopped paying me to work at her poncey bridal boutique. Economic climate, blah blah. There wasn't even a more-free-time silver lining to this tale of woe, cos I still worked there. I just didn't get paid. Was I a mug? Quite possibly.

'So. About Dylan . . .' said Donna. I watched her doing the gaping-mouth crazy-eyes-at-the-ceiling thing as she put in her contact lenses.

'Oh, riiight. So that's why you nearly trod on a dog on the way to school,' I said, not purposely avoiding the question.

Donna blinked and rubbed the corners of her eyes. 'Yeah, well. I overslept. And I'm not going out with my glasses on, am I?'

'You look lovely with your glasses on.'

She looked at me sceptically. 'Right.'

'Oop. Kettle boiling.' I went over to the scabby worktop and reached to get two mugs down from the cupboard. They were chipped and stained with months of dried-on tea, which, in this place, passed for sparkly clean. Teabag in each, splosh of milk (it was on the turn – again, it could have been worse), quick stir and squeeze, bags in the bin, and I was back in my scratchy-yet-squishy common-room chair ready to analyse Dylan. Not that there was much to analyse.

'Yeah. Fit,' I said airily, recalling his long legs and lush hair, and not exactly feeling what I'd describe as airy. 'If only he'd have stopped yakking. Couldn't get a word in.'

Donna laughed. 'I know. He was weird, no? Marv reckons he's just shy.'

So Donna had been talking about Dylan with her cousin. Did she like him? I got a sudden flash of the green-eyes, which I just as quickly pushed away.

'You fancied him though, right?' Don took a smug sip of tea. She knew me too well.

I shrugged. 'Out of my league, babes. I might as well fancy Robert Pattinson . . .' I paused. 'Uh, did you? Fancy him?' We didn't usually fancy the same type, but you never knew.

She wrinkled her nose. 'Nah. You know my rule about cardigans.'

'He wasn't wearing a cardigan!' I protested, although personally I like a boy in a floppy cardi. In my experience it's an item of knitwear that confounds stereotypes when worn by a boy, although obvs it has to be worn with the right amount of irony. Let it be known: cardi wearers are good in bed.

Don sniffed. 'Yeah, he was. Under the blazer.' She shook her head. 'Not my type . . . But *definitely yours* . . .' She sang the last two words.

I smiled. 'Like I said: out of my league.' It was gutting, really. All weekend after the cinema I'd kept thinking about him. I'd be watching telly or on the loo or trying to get to sleep and there he'd be, leaning nonchalantly against the wall of my mind, one skinny-jeaned leg crossed over the other. Well, that wasn't *all* he did. And lots of times he was naked.

Anyway.

'Don't be a pussy,' said Donna. 'You can have anyone you want. You've had most of the boys in this school, for example.' She smiled prettily. Bitch.

'Piss off,' I said merrily. 'And, anyway, there's a whole heap o' difference between them and . . . him. He's beautiful.'

Don put her hand on my knee and cocked her head earnestly. 'As are you, Ashley. As are you.'

I shoved her hand off. Very funny. 'Sasha's the beautiful one,' I said, draining my tea just as the beeps for next period went.

'Uh-huh.'

Donna could eye-roll all she wanted but the facts spoke for themselves. My perfect big sister was beautiful to my OK; good to my naughty; kind to my evil. *C'est*, unfortunately, *la vie*.

'Anyway, Marv reckons they're all coming to Ollie's party,' continued Donna as we paused at the door before she turned left to theatre studies and I turned right to media studies. 'You never know . . .'

Right. You never know . . . but you usually do. I put Dylan out of my mind and spent the next couple of hours working on my media studies coursework.

We had to make short documentaries. I was loving it. Like, really loving it. And, without wanting to sound like a complete wanker, there was a chance it could change my life. Unlike most of the others, I hadn't already started my uni applications. Donna wanted to be an actor; Cass was going for law at Cambridge, among others; Sarah wanted to do history of art; Ollie fancied music; Jack was going to do sports science . . . which left me and Rich floundering. I don't think Rich had a scooby what he wanted to do with his life and, until recently, neither did I. So I decided I wasn't going to go to uni. Not yet, anyway. It seemed kind of ridiculous to spend all that money on doing something I didn't care about just for the sake of getting a degree. Mum and Sasha were shocked and appalled, *bien sûr*, but it was my life. And, anyway, it had paid off: I'd found something I could be really passionate about. I'd done my research and I'd decided to apply to do film at Southampton, Bournemouth, Falmouth and East Anglia. As yet, nobody knew, and they never would unless I got a place. And I needed this documentary to complete my applications.

I'd decided to focus on people who'd had near-death experiences. This was a subject close to my thankfully still-beating heart, since I'd almost drowned swimming in the sea in Devon last half term. (Long story.) I thought using it for coursework might stop me having nightmares about it. It was kind of working. And, of course, Dylan had taken over my dreams for the past couple of nights, to *très* pleasing effect.

I'd already come up with a few real-life stories from local papers and crappy magazines, hidden among the stupid 'I Botoxed my armpits' and 'My husband's cheese fetish' sort of stories. One or two of them were right on the money. Reading their stories had made me realize just how dull mine was. I'd stopped breathing, then started again. End of. The time from when I got in the sea to when I woke up in hospital is just a blank. It's as if less than a second passed between the two events. But these people saw lights, watched themselves from above, lost all fear of death, etc. I wish I'd had all that.

I was engrossed in some old lady's story from the website of our local paper (about her house being bombed when she was a kid in the Second World War), when someone shoved my desk.

'Hey!' I said, ready to have a go, but it was just Sam. He didn't like me, although he used to. We'd once hooked up at a party. Truly, I'd never have gone there if I'd thought for a moment he *really* liked me. And the only reason I laughed when he told me he did was because I genuinely thought he was joking. Anyway, two years on and he still couldn't look at me without scowling. I tried a friendly smile, but he ignored me and walked to his desk, a book about Dungeons and Dragons under his arm. Mmm, sexy.

Dylan on the other hand . . .

Sod it. I had nothing to lose except my dignity, and that went long ago. Looking around quickly to check that Matt, our teacher, wasn't in sight, I logged on to Facebook. It was only a matter of time before school blocked it, but for now we were free to socially network to our hearts' content. Facebooking in class time, however, was a major no-no. We're talking withdrawal of Internet privileges. So I was furtive furtive, quickly finding Dylan in Marv's friend list and sending my own request. If he'd accepted it by the time I got home, I'd message him.

But first I had the rest of the day to get through. I had just enough time before the end of the lesson to fire off a quick email to the editor of the newspaper with a message for the old lady, asking her if she'd let me interview her about her experience, then I went along to the canteen for lunch, as always, and where, as always, Donna, Ollie, Jack and our other friends Sarah, Cass and Rich were sitting at the fourth table from the left, roughly in the middle of the room. Don't know why or how we'd picked that one – or even when – but on the rare occasions someone else was sitting there it was like walking into your bedroom and finding a stranger in your bed. And not in a good way.

'Still doing pack-ups?' asked Cass sympathetically, eyeing my hastily chucked together cheese-and-pickle sandwich, now limp after a morning in my bag. She hadn't bought lunch from the canteen either, but that was because she'd stopped at a deli on the way to school to pick up her usual £4 chicken-salad flatbread hold-the-mayo. She reckons it's because she doesn't like the crappy bread in the school sandwiches, and she has a point. But £4?

I nodded and took a bite of soggy bread and sweaty cheese. It was edible, anyway. And Cass didn't need to look so sorry for me. Mum still had the shop and the house. We weren't on benefits quite yet.

'So I hear you had a good weekend,' said Sarah,

peering at me saucily from behind her Ribena carton. 'Dylan was it . . . ?'

I shot daggers at Donna, who shrugged not at all guiltily. 'What? I didn't know it was a secret.'

That *what* was a secret? God, you admit to fancying one boy and it's Agatha Christie time.

'There's nothing to tell,' I said to Sarah. 'He's not for me.'

She shook her head. 'Ash, I have no doubt at all that you could have anyone you wanted . . . I've never yet seen a boy who doesn't fancy you.'

'Piss off!' I spluttered.

'It's true,' said Ollie seriously. 'I'd have you here and now if it was socially acceptable.'

'You'd have *anyone* here and now if it was socially acceptable,' I replied. 'No offence.'

He nodded amiably. 'Fair point.'

'But seriously, Ash,' said Rich, who was busy examining a spot on his chin using the mirror in Donna's eyeshadow compact. 'You really like him?'

I chucked my sandwich down on the table in mock outrage, where it instantly curled up at the edges like some fish corpse (the sandwich, not the outrage). 'What is this?' I demanded. 'You're never usually this interested in my love life.'

'That's cos *usually* you've already shagged them,' said Jack. 'This is new.'

Cheeky bastard. That's so not true, for the record. But all I said was: 'Yeah, well. He doesn't fancy me. End of.'

Dylan, Dylan, Dylan. If my friends hadn't made such a thing out of it I might have been able to put him out of my mind. But the bastards made sure he was installed good and proper, so by the time I got home that afternoon I was practically panting to get on the computer to check Facebook.

I slammed the front door and ran to the back room without taking my coat off, where, sitting straight-backed and serene at our computer, was my sister Sasha.

'What are you doing here?' I blurted. 'Why aren't you at work?' Fair questions. She didn't live at home any more, after all. And didn't she have a laptop/iPad/iPhone/other assorted shiny, portable Internet gadgets? The 'executive home' she shared with her 'partner' (vomit) Toby in Kent, with its mini 'guest toiletries' in the 'guest bedroom en suite' and its tasteful sofas and tastefully framed 'art' on the walls, was chock-full of the stuff. Technology coming out of its bright red-bricked ears. WiFi flowing invisibly from no less than three little blinking boxes attached neatly to the wall in the downstairs study, the loft room and in the garage. The garage FFS!

'Oh, hey, Ashley,' said Sasha, turning and smiling sweetly. 'I've got the day off. I've finally persuaded Mum to do her food shopping online so I'm signing her up with Ocado as it does Waitrose.' She turned back to the screen. 'It's by far the best, both ethically and in quality.'

Right. How fascinating. Kill me now if I'm going to find myself discussing supermarkets by the time I'm twenty-four. 'Well, are you going to be long? I need to use the computer.'

'About quarter of an hour?' said Sasha without turning round. 'I'll come and find you when I'm done.'

I made a face at her back and went into the kitchen to grab a snack. Monday wasn't one of Mum's shop's late-opening nights, but Mum still wouldn't be home till six, when we'd have pizza for tea. Monday-night ritual. On my way up to my room I stuck my head into the living room, where my little sister Frankie was watching TV. Most twelve-year-olds would be watching crappy American teeny sitcoms on the Disney Channel or something, but she was sat in the lotus position in front of Mum's yoga DVD.

'All right, Franks?'

She held up a finger to tell me to wait, then placed the tips of her middle finger and thumb together and brought them in front of her, just like the skinny bird in the leotard was doing on the screen, breathed in deeply and chanted a long, slow, 'Ommmmm.' Then she paused the screen and spun round to face me, her hand-me-down school shirt and navy pleated skirt about as un-yogary as you could get.

I raised an eyebrow. 'Good sesh?'

'Yeah, brilliant. Apart from all the farting.' She gave me an unwavering gaze – the only sort she does, my crazy sister – and I laughed.

'Mum says it happens all the time in her yoga class,' she said reproachfully.

'Sure it does, Frankie-pank,' I said. 'Good day?'

She turned back to the screen. 'It was OK. Miss Baines said I had an unusual talent for mimicry.'

'Who were you mimicking?'

She pulled her legs back into the lotus position. 'Miss Baines.'

Of course. I turned to go, then stopped and said, 'Do you know why Sasha's here? It can't just be for Mum's Internet shopping.'

Frankie sucked her teeth impatiently. 'Dunno. Maybe she's had a row with Toby.' She clicked the DVD off pause.

Interesting, although I doubted it was true. Toby and Sasha were disgusting together, all little kisses and 'sweetheart' and 'darling'. I left Frankie to her 'omming' and went up to my room to change.

Ah, my room. Sasha gave it to me when she left

home to go to uni. It was the best present she'd ever given me, by about a million miles. I'd spent a whole half term transforming it. I'd stripped off her Laura Ashley wallpaper and painted the whole room purple, except the dark-wood floorboards which I left as they were. Then I'd covered my bed with a couple of metres of this mental 1960s geometric-print fabric I'd found in Oxfam. I'd bought some slatted wooden blinds from Ikea and put those up in place of Sasha's gross floral curtains, and finally put my giant Kurt Cobain poster on the wall. There was nothing I could do about the disgusting fake-wood wardrobe – I couldn't afford a new one – so I'd moved it beside the door where at least you couldn't see it when you first came in. Who knew I was so creative? It was just how I'd imagined it, and I loved it. It was my space. I'd even put a bolt on the door, right up at the top so you wouldn't know it was there, although Mum had noticed almost straight away, with her mental mum-radar. I'd promised I'd never lock it at night, no sirree, so she let me keep it. Obviously I *had* locked it, but she'd never realized.

As always, the first thing I did when I got to my room was turn on my CD player, then close the blinds and turn on my bedside light. (I never used the ceiling light. I preferred to keep some things in the shadows. Deep, *non*?) Next, my school clothes were off and leggings and a mahoosive jumper were on.

Relief. I'd just flopped on to my bed for a bout of staring into space when Sasha knocked on my door and poked her head round.

'Computer's free, Ashy,' she cooed. For the record, I hate being called Ashy.

I jumped up from my bed and followed her out of the door. 'You off, then?' I asked. She shook her head, her blonde ponytail bobbing perkily.

'I brought a chicken casserole for supper. Thought Mum deserved a break, you know? Something tells me she doesn't get an awful lot of help when I'm not around.'

I stuck my tongue out at her back. 'Yes, well. Sorry to spoil your fun, but Monday's pizza night. And it's tea, not supper.'

She shrugged. 'Tea, supper. Same difference. And it won't kill you to eat a home-cooked meal on a Monday.'

'My point is,' I said, through gritted teeth, 'Mum doesn't need a break because making a two-minute phone call to order pizza is not exactly hard work.'

'*Whatever*,' sang Sasha, running lightly downstairs, her perfectly manicured nails skimming the banister. I bared my teeth at her as she went into the kitchen to do her good-daughter deed for the day, then I speedily veered off into the back room. I pressed a key to bring the screen to life and quickly logged on to Facebook, where my stomach did a little lurch cos Dylan had accepted my friend request. Whoop! I bashed out a quick message. Well, I say 'bashed'. I spent ten minutes agonizing over the perfect wordage to make it seem like I'd just bashed it out. I ended up with:

> Hey. Good to meet you the other night. Xmas party details: it's on Sat 3rd Dec at the football hut on Bishops Lane – I think Cubs meet there too, if that was ever your thing. Dib dib dib. Ashley.

Oh, be still my splitting sides. But it'd do. I squeezed my eyes shut and clicked SEND before I could change my mind. A glance at Dylan's profile told me there wasn't much to see. No status updates or timeline posts to speak of. I wasn't into revealing all on Facebook. Nice to know he had similar standards. I clicked on Info anyway, just to check, like, and almost laughed out loud when I saw his top music, films and TV programmes were pretty much a mirror for mine. You've got to respect a straight guy for having the guts to tell the world that one of his favourite movies is *The Wizard of Oz* (and I knew he was straight, before you go thinking otherwise, cos Donna had asked Marv), and I didn't know anyone else who dug *Question Time* like I did (it's totally *Jeremy Kyle* with brains).

Still smiling to myself, I opened another browser window and checked my emails. The editor of the newspaper had replied as well. Get me, all Ms Popular.

She told me her assistant had contacted the old lady, who'd be happy for me to get in touch. Result. Well, no time like the present, *carpe diem* and all that. I picked up my phone and keyed in the lady's phone number.

'Good afternoon. Bridget Harper speaking.' She had literally the poshest voice I'd ever heard. She could have given the Queen a run for her money in the cut-glass stakes.

I cleared my throat. 'Oh hi, my name's Ashley. I think the editor of –'

But she interrupted me. 'Oh yes, hello there. You wanted to interview me about the war for a school project?'

Whoa, no flies on her. She must have been about ninety, but from her voice you'd think she was thirty years younger.

'Yes, if that's OK.'

'Of course. It'll make a nice change. Daytime television is not exactly uplifting.'

Hilarious. I arranged to go to her house ('I assume you're not an axe murderer, dear?') after school in a couple of days, and then quickly ended the call because – *ping!* – I had a reply from Dylan.

Hmm. Was he keen or just efficient? I opened the message with my heart doing little skipettes.

I'll be there! Dylan x

And there, *mes amis*, is the definition of short and sweet. Beaming like an idiot and with jumping beans getting jiggy in my stomach, I texted Donna:

> Guess who just messaged
> me on fb??

True to form, she called back within approximately 2.8 seconds.

'Told you he liked you.'

I shut down the computer and jogged back up the stairs to my room. I flopped on to my bed, but was too fidgety. I got up and started pacing instead. 'Don't get excited. He just said he was coming to the party . . . Maybe he fancies *you*.'

She snorted. 'Get off. You know he doesn't.'

'Well, I'm not counting any chickens, babes, but I'll give it a go.'

'Good girl,' she said. 'So what did his message say, exactly?' And we spent the next twenty minutes until Mum got home from work and called me for tea analysing those four words and an x till they were pretty much imprinted on my very soul. It was all good.

FOR FICTION TO MAKE YOU

GASP out loud
STAY up late *and*
MISS your stop